"Are your questions professional or personal?" he asked, his eyes roaming from her heaving chest to her full lips, to stare into her eyes.

Francine's heart started racing, and her mouth suddenly went very dry as she leaned her head back in order to maintain eye contact. "Depends," she said, her voice barely above a whisper.

"On what, exactly?" Meeks whispered as he lowered his head, slowly rubbing his nose along her cheek before capturing her mouth, giving her a slow, gentle kiss that sent shock waves through her body.

The kiss turned deep and purposeful. His hands found her hair clip and rele___ ___ ___ ___ ___ fall over his long fi___

Francine was overw___ ___ his kiss.

Meeks raised his he___ ___ ___ ___ ___ ___ s desire-filled eyes. "I've wanted to do that all night," he said before taking her lips again. He released her again but only long enough to add, "Truth be told, I've wanted to do that for years."

Right or wrong, Francine wanted Meeks in this moment more than she'd ever wanted anything in her life. Pushing aside all doubt and fear from her mind, she slid her arms up and around his neck. "Is that all you've wanted to do?" she asked, kissing the corner of his jaw.

"Hell no," he said, his voice deep and commanding. Meeks swept Francine off her feet. "And tonight's only the beginning."

Dear Reader,

When I sat down and penned the first book in The Blake Sisters series, I knew I wanted it to be fun and sexy and send a clear message. What message? Well, I'm going to leave that up to you to figure out.

As a lifelong fan of romance, Harlequin books in particular, I enjoy reading and writing stories that infuse an element of intrigue with the pursuit of romance. In *Protecting the Heiress*, the struggle between Francine and Meeks as they balance their business relationship with a budding personal one is sexy and intense. The constant battles that often exist in these relationships make the emotional roller-coaster ride much more thrilling.

I thoroughly enjoy interacting with readers, so please let me know how you enjoyed Francine and Meeks's story. You can email me at Kennerson94@comcast.net or contact me on Facebook or Twitter. I look forward to bringing you middle sister Farrah Blake's story very soon.

So until next time,

Martha

PROTECTING
the HEIRESS

MARTHA
KENNERSON

HARLEQUIN® KIMANI™ ROMANCE

Recycling programs
for this product may
not exist in your area.

ISBN-13: 978-0-373-86416-4

Protecting the Heiress

Copyright © 2015 by Martha Kennerson

HARLEQUIN®

Printed in U.S.A.

www.Harlequin.com

Martha Kennerson's love of reading and writing is a significant part of who she is, and she uses both to create the kinds of stories that touch your heart. Martha lives with her family in League City, Texas, and believes her current blessings are only matched by the struggle it took to achieve such happiness. To find out more about Martha and her journey, check out her website at marthakennerson.com.

Books by Martha Kennerson

Harlequin Kimani Romance

Protecting the Heiress

Visit the Author Profile page at Harlequin.com for more titles.

This book is dedicated to my family and friends.
It was their love and support that gave me the courage
to go after my lifelong dream to write for Harlequin
and for that I'm truly grateful.

Chapter 1

Francine Blake walked past the midlevel cubicles and glass office doors, smiling and speaking to everyone she passed.

"Morning, Francine. Great job last night. I know it was supposed to be work, but I had a blast covering security for the mayor's party," Jay said, giving her a wide smile.

It had been the first time that Francine had worked with the junior agent. She returned his smile. "Thanks, you did a great job, too."

Francine Blake was a partner in her family's twenty-five-year-old multibillion-dollar international security firm and private detective agency based in Houston, Texas, which specialized in both corporate and personal matters for elite clientele. Francine, a security specialist who also had a degree in forensic science, had joined the firm five years earlier as a field agent and within the past year had taken over as its chief executive officer—responsible for the sales and administrative aspects of the organization—after her father's retirement, into which his family had forced him after a major health scare.

"I emailed the detailed summary report of last night's activities out to everyone, and I included all the pictures." Jay started walking toward the elevators.

"Wait, you attached *all* the pictures?" she asked with a slight hitch in her voice.

"Yeah, why?" he replied as he pushed the down button on the elevator.

"No reason. Have a nice day and stay safe out there," Francine said as she watched Jay enter the elevator.

Francine sighed and gave her head a slow shake. It had been quite a while since the twenty-eight-year-old had to play a role in the field in such a dynamic fashion and while she'd had a blast doing it, she didn't relish the grief she knew was coming: having to explain her actions to her father, Meeks and other board members who still didn't completely trust her judgment. While Francine had always secretly lusted after her extremely handsome business partner Meeks Montgomery and his beautiful body, their close connection prevented them from exploring anything beyond a friendship. She turned and continued on toward the conference room, only to be stopped again. This time, it was one of their office researchers.

"Dang, girl, I saw the pictures from last night's party. You wore the heck out of that dress," the pretty young researcher said, giving Francine a half smile and a raised eyebrow.

"It was work," Francine protested.

"Whatever, looked like a party to me. Anyway, where did you get that dress, and did it come in any other colors?" she asked.

Francine ignored her question. "Who else saw the pictures?" she asked, unable to hide the surprise in her voice.

In that moment, she could feel Meeks, standing nearby, staring at her. Their connection was like a heat-seeking missile whenever they were in the same room. A fact that wasn't hard to miss. Francine cut her gaze to the cubicle where Meeks and his assistant Jeremy stood, clearly listening to their conversation.

The young researcher tilted her head and frowned. "We all did, and I have to say, if you ever decide to give up this CEO gig, I know a high-end modeling agency I could hook you up with," she said as she walked off laughing.

"Great, just great," Francine murmured to herself as she walked past the cubicle where all the guys were congregating. She ignored Meeks's smug look, but before she could make it across the threshold of the conference room, she was handed a cup of espresso and a manila folder by a pretty but obviously nervous blonde she'd never seen before.

"Here's your espresso with extra milk just like you like it, and the client information you requested, Ms. Blake."

Francine was about to introduce herself when she heard another voice behind her. "Cine, I think that's meant for me. Thanks, Kelly," Farrah said, walking toward her sister.

Francine turned to greet her, only to be taken aback by what she saw. Farrah was dressed in the same company uniform that Francine was wearing—black cargo pants, a black fitted T-shirt with the company's red-and-black logo and combat boots, except that her hair was pulled back into a low ponytail. It was like looking into a mirror—almost. The Blake triplets were near identical except for their eye color. However, it had been a long time since she and Farrah had actually dressed alike.

Francine rolled her eyes skyward in acknowledgment of the confusion. "Farrah, what's with the outfit?"

"What are you talking about?" she questioned, looking down at herself.

"What am I talking about? You're dressed like one of our agents instead of a lawyer—the head of our legal department. I thought you had an appointment at the courthouse today," Francine said, gesturing to her sister's outfit. "And we both know you can't go to court dressed like that."

"Oh, that," she answered with a shrug. "The appointment had to be rescheduled. So I decided to go out with one of the guys later for a ride-along," Farrah explained as she walked past her sister and toward Kelly, who was standing against the glass wall looking like she'd just been hit by a stun gun.

"Wait, you're going on a ride-along...why?" Francine asked with raised eyebrows. She changed directions and tried to catch up with her younger sister. "You're not assigned to any cases and your security certification doesn't expire for another couple of months. Besides, I thought you were going to sit in on the client meeting with me."

Farrah faced her sister, sighed and said, "I will, calm down. Danny invited me to ride out with him, so I'm taking him up on his offer and getting the field assessment out of the way, since my workload is relatively light at the moment." Farrah took several sips of her espresso before she continued. "Danny's still responsible for doing the recertifications, right?"

Meeks, as the company's chief operations officer, was responsible for all aspects of the firm's day-to-day security operations, and usually handled all the certifications for the executives personally. However, lately, he'd been relinquishing some of his administrative duties to Danny, one of his senior security agents, in favor of spending more time in the field. Francine knew this had everything to do with the recent injury she'd received as a result of her taking the lead on a case and his overprotective attitude toward her, just like when they were kids. Even if they were outside playing or working out in the company's gym, Meeks was always around, keeping a watchful eye out on her and her sisters; first it had been as a favor to their father, then it just became his norm.

"Danny should be able to take care of it," Francine said as they stood next to the conference room door.

"Great!" Farrah turned to face Kelly and said, "Kelly, this is my oldest sister and our company's chief executive officer, Francine Blake. Cine, this is Kelly. She's our new intern. She'll be covering for Paul while he's on his honeymoon with John."

Francine extended her hand to Kelly. "Sorry about the confusion. I guess my sister forgot to tell you she—"

"Had an identical twin," Kelly supplied, offering Francine a trembling hand to shake.

"Actually, there are three of them," Meeks said. He walked toward Kelly with his hand extended. He also wore the resident uniform—a practice most employees followed, unless an assignment, client or event called for otherwise—but it looked much sexier on him. "Meeks Montgomery. Ms. Ross, is it?"

Kelly dropped Francine's hand as though it were diseased and quickly accepted Meeks's. The confused expression quickly faded and was replaced with a look of adoration, aimed at Meeks's athletically built six-foot-tall frame, with smooth caramel skin, full lips and a bright smile, surrounded by a perfectly manicured goatee. His Greek god–like appearance was breathtaking.

"Yes," Kelly replied, barely holding in her giggle.

Farrah rolled her eyes and sighed. "Kelly, Meeks is our chief operations officer and resident heartthrob, so keep in mind that you can look, but don't touch," she said, laughing.

"Farrah," Francine said, giving her sister a look that was clearly some type of warning.

Ignoring her sister with a dismissive wave of her hand, Farrah said, "Oh, don't worry. He'll never make a move on you." She shrugged. "I just don't want you to get your hopes up, start fantasizing about having a bunch of little Meekses, get your heart broken and go all crazy. Besides, everyone knows his heart belongs to—"

"Farrah, that's enough!" Francine said in a forceful tone that caught her sister off guard.

"Don't we have a client meeting soon?" Meeks offered. Farrah raised her eyebrows and fell silent. He turned to a flustered Kelly and said, "Nice to meet you, Ms. Ross. Welcome aboard," before walking into the conference room.

"Nice, sis," Francine leaned over to whisper, trying not to smile at her sister's antics.

"I thought so," she whispered back.

"You are a mess," Francine said, walking past her sister.

Chapter 2

Francine walked into the conference room where she found Mary Walker, their office manager, and Robert Gold, the head of the field security agents and Meeks's right-hand man, waiting for her to arrive.

Robert had folded his six-foot frame into a chair at the ten-seat mahogany conference table. He was reading over a client's preliminary information. His mirrored Armani sunglasses covered his piercing blue eyes. The fair skin of his square jaw was covered by a five-o'clock shadow.

"Another long night, Robert?" Francine asked mockingly.

Robert simply nodded his response. "But not as long as yours. And by the looks of these pictures, not quite as fun either," Robert said, flipping through pages on his tablet.

"Don't!" Francine warned. "You'd swear you'd never seen a woman in a minidress and heels before. It was perfectly appropriate for the occasion."

Robert raised his hands in surrender.

"Robert and I only have twenty minutes before we have another meeting, so shall we get started?" Meeks asked, looking around the room.

Francine and her sister took their seats next to Mary. Francine always found it difficult to sit across from Meeks. His take-charge attitude, handsome face and sexy smile were distracting—at least until he opened his arrogant mouth.

"First order of business, we're going to pass on this client. We don't need to deal with a celebrity of this magnitude," Meeks said with a note of finality in his voice as he glared at Francine.

Francine met his glare before saying, "Seriously? You're going to take it there?"

Farrah's brow creased, and she looked back and forth between Meeks and Francine before asking, "What's going on, Cine?"

Francine pushed out a slow breath before responding. "Meeks is tripping about my stepping in to cover for Karen last night," Francine explained to her sister.

"What…why? Did something happen? Cine, you know what the doctor said!"

"Not you too, Farrah," she said, reaching for one of the bottles of water that sat in the center of the table. "I'm fine and no, nothing happened. Besides, it was just a party."

"Yeah, a party that went all night," Meeks said. His hand brushed against Francine's retreating arm as he too reached for a bottle of water, their eyes meeting instantly. "And one where you had to physically remove two people by yourself, which is why I suspect you were hurting so bad when you got in this morning."

Francine glared at Meeks through narrowed eyes, which she hoped expressed just how mad she was about his over-sharing as she took a sip of her water. She was trying to extinguish the fire his touch had ignited in the lower half of her body. He had obviously read the required incident report, but he'd failed to mention that she had handled things smoothly and hadn't triggered any alerts on her tracking device. Anyone working in the field was required to wear a tracking watch. If necessary, all the agent had to do was push a button, should they need assistance.

"Did you really have to tell all that?" she challenged.

"Maybe your sister can talk some sense into you, since I obviously can't."

The room was quiet for several moments as the sisters stared at each other.

"It really wasn't…" Francine said.

Farrah nodded. "…that serious, I get it, but—"

"You're right, it could have been worse, but it wasn't," Francine declared.

"But…" Farrah stared at her sister.

"They're doing that weird twin-triplet communication thing again," Robert whispered to Mary.

"Hush up," she replied, smacking Robert on his arm.

"All right, I might have overdone it a little last night," Francine conceded.

Farrah tilted her head and raised her left eyebrow.

"All right, I overdid it a lot, but I wasn't in any danger. Happy now?" she asked her sister.

"And?" Farrah nudged.

"And I won't do it again. Can we move on? We do have a client coming," she said, glaring at Meeks as she flipped through the pages on her tablet with far more gusto then she intended. Francine hated to feel like she was being scolded by anyone, but especially by one of her sisters. She was just thankful that Felicia was on the other side of the world; otherwise, as the doctor in the family, she'd demand to give her a physical exam.

"As I said, I think we should pass on this one," Meeks reiterated. "Surely there are other less notable celebrities we could use for this...test."

Like hell, buster! Keep it professional, Francine. After Francine gave herself a quick pep talk on the best way to handle the situation, her eyes searched the room before landing on Meeks. "While I appreciate your concern and input, we *won't* be passing. I've already advised Mr. Morgan of that fact and accepted his *very large* retainer, so unless Robert's found something in his background check..." Francine paused long enough to give Robert time to respond.

Robert looked at Meeks, then back at Francine before he reluctantly said, "Nothing that sends up any red flags. Daniel's team is available, so if we're taking the job, we're ready to go."

"That's great. Let's move forward." Francine shot Meeks another look that challenged him to say anything.

He didn't.

"Now, I know Daniel and his team are some of the best guys we have, but I promised Mr. Morgan that I'd stay close to things, so I'm taking the lead on this one."

"Hell, no!" Meeks declared, slamming both hands of the table.

Everyone froze and stared at him. "Excuse me?" Francine said, her eyebrows standing at attention.

"How many times *do* you need to be shot to get it through that beautiful stubborn head of yours that—"

"That what?" she asked, thrusting her chin forward. "We're not kids that need your protection anymore. You do know that, right?"

Before he could say anything else, there was a knock on the conference room door just before Kelly flung it open.

"Excuse me, Mr. Morgan and Tiffany...*the* Tiffany... just arrived," she said in an excited voice.

"Looks like our young intern is starstruck...and a little fickle, too," Robert said, laughing from behind his sunglasses.

"Robert," Mary scolded, hitting his arm again.

"They're not supposed to be here for another hour," Francine protested, glaring at her sister. "You forgot to have Paul reschedule the appointment, didn't you?"

"May...be," she said, giving her sister a sheepish look that a little kid would give when they knew they'd done something wrong. "Look, there was a lot going on with planning the wedding and all."

"It was Paul's wedding, not yours." Francine reminded.

Robert smiled at Farrah.

"I...I mean, he's basically the brother we never had, and he needed my help. We paid for it," Farrah declared.

"Again...still not your wedding."

Farrah laughed.

"They sent them up from the lobby, so I put them in the VIP lounge," Kelly said.

Tiffany Tanner was the current big thing in entertainment—a young starlet whose most recent movie had made millions within hours of its opening. She was beautiful, rich and a household name, which made her need for a bodyguard a no-brainer. What was strange was her immediate need for a complete security overhaul.

"Please show our guests to the conference room next to my office," Francine said. "Thanks, Kelly."

After Kelly closed the door behind her, Francine focused on Meeks. "We *are* taking this case. The board agreed to this trial period for celebrity personal protection and it's my job to select which celebrity we'll be working with. We're just fortunate that Tiffany was looking for a new agency. Daniel's team will be assigned, and Farrah and I will be taking the lead. Any questions?" She gave him no time to respond. "Good!"

Francine stood, collected her things and said to her sister, "Shall we?" She gave Meeks a parting nod before she swept out of the room.

"Right behind you, sis," Farrah said. She looked at Meeks, smiled and said, "I guess she told you."

"One of you might want to change your hairstyle or something so the client will be able to tell you apart," Meeks said before they cleared the table.

Farrah unbound her hair, bowed her head and shook out her long curls. She rose up, fluffed her hair with her fingers and smiled.

Robert lowered his sunglasses and said, "Damn!"

Farrah laughed, winked at Robert and left the room.

Chapter 3

Damn, man, you sound like a girl! Meeks chided himself for the hair comment.

He remained at the conference table, fuming at the ridiculousness of it all. He was reluctant to contradict Cine, as his earlier outburst had surprised everyone—including himself. Was the woman trying to get herself killed?

It was bad enough that that bastard Raymond Daniels—a former enemy who blamed Francine for his arrest—came gunning for her even when he was out on bond. *Too bad the cops got to him and put him back in jail before I got ahold of him. Does she have to keep putting herself in dangerous situations?* Meeks thought as he picked up his tablet and phone.

When the board approved the expansion of the personal protection division to include celebrities, Meeks had tried to keep an open mind. However, the clients they assisted other agencies with only confirmed his worst fears, and Meeks was determined to change the board's mind. Meeks was already having problems with the personal protection division since Francine insisted on continuing her field-work; adding celebrity to that mix only enhanced his resolve to eliminate the line completely.

While personal protection for celebrities had the potential to become an extremely profitable piece of business, it brought a lot of unnecessary chaos—unwanted publicity, uncooperative clients and questionable situations—chaos Meeks felt that their already extremely profitable agency could do without. However, Francine's desire and ability to expand that line of business, ultimately increasing their profits expediently in a short period of time, had made that goal a lot more difficult. Now keeping Francine out of harm's way was his new priority. If he again allowed Mr. Blake's daughter to be seriously injured—or even worse—on his watch, Meeks would never forgive himself.

"Well, I guess that means the meeting's adjourned," Robert proclaimed as he pushed his glasses back up his nose and stood.

Meeks followed Robert out the door when Mary said, "Not so fast, you two."

Both men stopped where they stood and gave her their undivided attention.

Mary Walker had worked for the company for over twenty-five years, but she had been a close friend to the Blakes even longer. She had been their father's assistant almost from the beginning, and her eldest daughter had even been the family's go-to babysitter for the triplets. Mary was promoted to office manager right after Meeks had joined the firm, taking his father's position upon his death, and had been like a second mother to him—to all of the staff, in fact.

She was small in stature, but her quiet strength and no-

nonsense attitude made her an unstoppable force. When Mary spoke, Meeks listened.

Mary tossed her salt-and-pepper hair from her shoulders, stood to her full five-foot height and placed her hands on her hips. "Francine was right. I know it's hard to believe, but the Blake women are strong and smart and can handle themselves," she pointed out. "You don't need to treat them like fragile dolls that need your constant supervision and protection. Your day of acting as their quasi bodyguard is over."

Meeks smiled and raised his hands with palms facing Mary, a sign of surrender. "Mary, I was only trying to—"

"I know what you were doing. You've been doing it for years and you need to find another way to do it. Try the direct approach," she advised, giving him a wide smile.

Mary was in her sixties, but with her caramel-colored skin still smooth and free of wrinkles, she looked twenty years younger and beautiful as ever. She picked up her coffee cup and files and left the men staring after her as she exited the conference room.

Meeks headed to his office without making eye contact with anyone he passed. His robotic movements, deep frown and tight jaw sent a clear message: *Leave me the hell alone.* He walked into his office and slammed the door behind him, but before he could even make it around his desk, his door opened, and there Robert stood.

"What?" Meeks snapped. He always held his tongue with Mary, but he didn't have to with Robert.

"Don't shoot," Robert said, raising his hands in mock surrender.

Meeks and Robert had been best friends since college, and at times, Meeks had been closer to Robert than his own brother. Robert and Meeks had started a technology company after graduation, and within a few years they'd sold it and made millions. With no concrete plans after the sale, Robert had agreed to join Meeks when he took over for his father after his death. While Meeks trusted Robert with his life and valued his opinions above most, he wasn't in the mood for any of them at the moment.

"Don't you have some work to do?" Meeks asked.

"Why don't you two just get together already?" Robert asked as he folded his arms and leaned against the doorframe. "If nothing else, maybe you'll get it out of your system."

"What are you talking about?" Meeks asked as he sat in his chair behind his father's antique cherrywood desk.

"You and Francine. You two have been doing this dance for a while now." He pushed off the doorframe and entered the office, closing the door behind him. "First, you said she was too young for you. Then she's the boss's daughter—"

"She's always been the boss's daughter," he declared.

"Then she's basically you in a dress. There's always something… In reality, you're crazy about her. Hell, we all know you're crazy about her. So do something about it already!"

"Cine and I are business partners. Period."

Robert took the seat directly across from Meeks's desk. "Which is why you were willing to walk away from a multimillion-dollar client? Because there was a remote possibility that Francine could be in danger?"

"Francine is the CEO of this company—an organization with a stellar worldwide reputation, which we all have worked hard for," he said, stabbing his index finger into his desk. "This was a role she was groomed and destined for. Hell, she's wanted it her whole life. She has no business working cases in the damn field. Didn't we learn that lesson last year when she was almost shot by that irate husband we helped put away?" he yelled at his friend. "Or how about two months ago when she *did* get shot?" He threw up his hands. "She could have died, for Christ's sake."

"Yeah, but she didn't, and working cases is *her* choice… not yours," he said, pointing at his friend. "Francine has been following in her father's footsteps since she was a kid. Do you remember telling me that? We both know she's more than qualified. Her and her sisters' years of martial arts training from not only their father, but from several experts in the field, set them apart from most. They're double black belts. Hell, Francine's better at handling herself and a weapon—any type of weapon too, gun, knife, crossbow—than some of the men we have walking around here," Robert said as he ran the back of his hand along his jawline. "Shit, if that asshole didn't get the jump on her, she wouldn't have gotten shot."

Meeks stood and turned to stare out his windows. "Being better than some of the men around here didn't stop her from getting shot now, did it? She could have died, man."

"So this *is* about your personal feelings for Francine, and not her abilities as an agent or her position with the company?"

Meeks glared at Robert over his shoulder.

"Because if it is," Robert tilted his head slightly, raised his eyebrows and pointed at him, "you ought to remember that danger is something we all face regularly. In fact, we all happily signed up for it, and Francine was the most eager of us all—a fact that we all knew from the first day she started working in the field five years ago."

"Yeah, I remember," Meeks mumbled, returning to his desk. "She was determined to show everyone that she was just as good as the men," he admitted grudgingly. "Turns out she was better than most of them, too."

Robert threw back his head and laughed. "We had to rethink our stance on a number of things, and she challenged us every step of the way. Remember when she insisted that everyone learn the 'art,'" he said, using air quotes to emphasize his point. "...of handling knives and bows and arrows?"

"Yeah, or when they both had all the men learn some form of martial arts because they thought that boxing shouldn't be the only hand-to-hand defense they knew." Meeks smiled as he remembered Big Bob trying to master the roundhouse kick. He was surprised just how well the large man had handled that three-hundred-pound body of his.

"There's not one thing she and Farrah can't do. You do realize that Francine is the reason why the team is as strong as it is today, right?"

"I know. I just..." Meeks's mind drifted for a moment.

Robert studied his friend before saying, "You know what happened with Jasmine wasn't your fault—or Francine for that matter...right? You surround yourself with a lot of strong women, and you can't blame yourself when they put themselves in harm's way and end up getting hurt. You can't protect them from themselves."

"Don't go there," Meeks warned. The last thing he wanted was to be reminded how he'd let his relationship with Jasmine blind him to her reckless ambition, something he swore he'd never let happen again. "This has nothing to do with Jasmine. With regard to Cine, I'd be just as concerned about any of our agents if they acted as recklessly as she did last night," he protested, all the while knowing his argument held no weight.

"Reckless? According to the debrief summary she did an excellent job—especially under the circumstances," Robert countered.

"And hurt herself in the process, too," Meeks shot back. "Not to mention, she had no backup."

Robert stood and headed for the door. "Damn, man. It was a party! She had plenty of backup on the scene. Everyone wore those new alert watches that you insist we all needed." He cracked open the door but gave a parting shot. "Our teams are the best at what they do, and they always have each other's backs, especially when it comes to working with the Blake sisters. And working with Cine in particular, you *always* have to be on point."

"Enough already, I get it. You think she's a superhero," Meeks said with a slight curve of his lips.

"Be careful. You don't want to feel the wrath of those Blake women," Robert said, giving his friend a half smile.

"Like you did with Farrah two months ago when she accused you of honing in on the Boyd case?" Meeks questioned.

"Exactly like that, especially since I wasn't honing in on anything, remember? You *sent* me to Vegas to keep an eye on her just to prevent Francine from having to go do it. Man, was Farrah pissed." Robert ran the back of his hand across his face.

"I wouldn't put it exactly like that," Meeks said, defending his choice to send Robert to Las Vegas so Francine wouldn't feel the need to go. "I never did find out what happened between you two while you were there."

"She didn't need or want my help, but we got the job done anyway, and that's all that matters. Besides, you know what they say. What happens in Vegas…" Robert laughed as he left Meeks's office.

Meeks knew his friend was right. The Blake women had been trained by their father, former army ranger Frank Blake, and by all accounts, he was the best in the business. He'd been determined to build the best security organization in the country. He had every intention of making sure his girls were prepared to take over and ensure his legacy when the time was right. Still, Meeks knew firsthand that no matter how well you'd been trained and groomed, accidents happened and there were some things that were beyond your control. He would be damned if he let something happen to Francine Blake.

Chapter 4

Francine walked into her office with Farrah right behind her. She now held the corner office that had once been occupied by their father. It was as large as the living room in her apartment and full of happy memories captured in the many photographs plastered on every wall between expensive works of art. The oval-shaped mahogany-wood-and-glass-topped desk that she'd designed and made herself sat in the center of the room atop a rich, earth-toned Persian rug that spoke more to Francine's style than the desk that had previously been used by their father.

While Francine may have hated her father's old desk, she loved his soft leather wingback chair and matching sofa, so they both stayed. But the possession of her father's that Francine prized the most was his massive book collection, a collection which was full of original works and first editions, along with several technical books that she reached for daily.

"Can you believe Meeks? Making this whole new cli-

ent thing about me…about my being shot?" Francine complained as she began pacing the floor of her office. "Like
I'm some helpless child that needs her hand held. What,
I'm suddenly too fragile to handle myself? I did my time
in the shrink's chair after the shooting, at Dad's insistence,
mind you, and I've had no lingering effects. I was cleared
to return to work. I don't need Meeks trying to tell me
what to do, too."

Farrah smiled and sat quietly on the sofa.

"I mean, it's not like I'm not capable of handling myself," she said, making tracks across the plush carpet.
"How many times have I laid his ass out during our work-
outs?"

Farrah crossed her legs and shot her sister a knowing
look, and her smile grew wider.

"Okay, maybe he did let me win," she conceded, "but
he's not your average man, either."

"He's not?" Farrah asked.

Francine stopped midstride and glared at her sister.
"Farrah, aren't you going to say anything about his be-
havior?"

"You don't want to hear what I have to say, and you
know it," she said, crossing her arms under her breasts.

Francine rolled her eyes to the ceiling, released a deep
breath and went to join her sister on the sofa. "What am I
going to do about Meeks?" Francine asked as she laid her
head on her sister's shoulder.

"I told you what to do. Invite him up to your place for
dinner and when he arrives, greet him wearing nothing
but your combat boots. Channel your inner Miley…better
yet, Beyoncé," she said, laughing as she swerved her hips.

"What?" Francine asked, trying not to laugh.

"When's the last time you had a little fun, anyway?"
she asked.

Francine threw her head back and laughed so hard she could barely catch her breath. Farrah had always been the wild one out of the three of them; she had inherited her adventurous spirit from their father. She was beautiful and wasn't afraid to admit that her looks could easily get her whatever she wanted. While all three triplets were brilliant overachievers, Farrah knew the fair skin and high cheekbones they inherited from their Italian mother and the luxurious jet-black hair, straight nose and chin they got from their African-American and Hispanic father gave her a superficial advantage against which she constantly had to fight.

"Thanks but I think I'll pass. And my sex life is not a topic up for discussion." Francine got up and returned to her desk. "Have you talked to Dad yet?" she asked.

Francine took a chocolate-covered almond Hershey's Kiss from the crystal candy dish that sat on her desk. At the same time, her sister pulled out a half-eaten candy bar from her purse and took a bite.

"You're still reaching for the chocolate whenever you get upset, I see," Farrah said.

"Right back at you," Francine replied, pointing to her sister's candy bar.

"Nope, I save the ice cream for that. Right now, I'm just hungry," Farrah said, biting into the bar.

"Whatever. About Dad…" Francine asked again.

"Yeah, I talked to him. You know, I never knew Dad could be so…so, I don't even know," she said, her voice rising several octaves.

"Farrah!" Francine hit the top of her desk with the palm of her hand. "Focus and tell me what happened."

"Meeks is what happened. He and Robert, in fact," she said.

"What?" Francine asked, throwing up her hands.

"They talked to Dad and—"

"When?"

"I'll tell you if you stop interrupting me," she said before taking another bite of her candy.

Francine closed her mouth, took her thumb and index finger and imitated turning an invisible lock on her lips. She then threw the imaginary key over her shoulder and glared at her sister.

"Thank you," Farrah said. "Anyway, thanks to Meeks and Robert, Dad all of a sudden agreed that personal security for celebrities brought on too much risk. And before you break that lock and ask, yes, I reminded him of just how much revenue that part of our business has generated over the last two years, and that expanding to work with celebrities was the next natural step." Farrah crossed her arms and legs. "I even reminded him that both Robert and Meeks were in favor of this division change until you got shot. We all know Meeks is making this personal when it should be about business. Mom has managed to keep Dad at bay for now, but if he manages to get the board to reconsider their decision and calls for a vote, we're screwed."

Francine had been able to convince her dad and the majority of the stockholders to give her one major celebrity client to prove that not only was this additional line of business profitable, but it also brought no extra danger to their team. Francine had been well on her way to selecting and perusing that client before she was shot. Fortunately Tiffany's case had landed in her lap at the perfect opportunity.

"Damn! If that didn't convince him, I'm not sure what will." Francine sat forward, crossed her arms on her desk and laid down her head. "If we can't convince Dad to change his mind, then we'll be at a shareholder stalemate."

"And let me remind you, sister dear, if that happens, the issue goes to the board for a decision." Farrah laughed and slowly shook her head. "Dad may not be an attorney, but he sure as hell thinks like one. Making that thirteen-person board full of his friends, which he virtually controls, have the final say in any decisions that the six shareholders can't resolve was brilliant."

Francine raised her head. "Just one more thing you got from Dad," Francine said.

Farrah smiled and flipped her hair. "What, my brilliance?"

Francine shook her head. "No, your sneakiness. So what do we do?" she asked, sitting up to reach for more candy.

"While I'm looking for some legal loopholes, you need to see how many board members you can convince to vote our way."

"Well, there are thirteen votes, and the six shareholders are split down the middle." Francine used her fingers to count off the votes. "So, of the outstanding seven members, I know we have Mom, Mary and Paul on our side. We either need to find a way to convince shareholder Matthew—"

"Not going to happen. Matthew always votes with Meeks…they're brothers," Farrah said.

"*Or*, we see if we can get one of Dad's old business cronies or one of those Army Special Forces kids to take back their voting proxy and vote our way," Francine countered.

"All right, what about his former business partner, the one who never leaves his house? What's his name? Bass, Brick?"

"It's Beck, Ronald Beck, but he'll never go against Dad," Francine said. "He and Eddie Mercado helped with the start-up funds for the business, remember? Dad's made them a fortune. Hell, he's made everybody a fortune."

"So which of the remaining two board members, those Special Forces kids, do you think you could have a shot with—Dallas Walls or James Grayson?" Farrah asked.

"Neither. Their fathers were a part of Dad's Special Forces group and he's had their proxies for years. I don't think either of them has ever even personally attended a board meeting. They run their own billion-dollar companies, after all," Francine said.

"You're right. Walls has that massive cattle ranch where he raises horses, and he also runs a string of steak houses. And Grayson owns the Grayson & Grayson Oil consortium with his sister. We're just a blip on their radar."

"Well, they inherited their seats from their dads. It's not like it was something they sought out to do. What's the deal with that, anyway?" Francine asked with a deep frown.

Farrah sat up straighter in her chair. "We're a privately owned company and we can set up the board any way we want. As long as we stick to our established bylaws, we can—"

"That's not what I mean, legal eagle," Francine said, rolling her eyes. "I never really understood why Dad gave two seats on the board to the kids of two men that died before he even started the company."

"According to Mom, Dad felt like he owed them. It's a ranger thing. So, any ideas?" Farrah asked.

"Actually, Mom might be able to convince Mr. Mercado," she said shyly.

Farrah's eyes widened, and she nodded slowly.

Francine's mother had told her girls that once upon a time, Eddie Mercado had had a crush on her. They'd even gone on a few dates before she'd met their father. Francine felt like it would be disloyal to her father to even ask her mother to approach the man themselves, even though her mother had assured them that their father had gotten past it years ago. They and Eddie had been friends and even business partners for years.

"Do you think Mom would do that?" Farrah asked,

frowning. "I mean, voting against Dad with us is one thing. Going to an old boyfriend for help to do it is something different entirely."

"What other choice do we have?"

"Anything but that. You know, if you'd just take Meeks to bed, we wouldn't be in this mess," Farrah said, laughing and making her eyebrows dance.

Francine sighed. "If only it were that easy. Besides, Meeks has made it perfectly clear that the only interest he has in me is professional."

Farrah threw her candy wrapper into the silver trash bin that sat at the corner of her sister's desk. "You couldn't tell that by his behavior, especially lately. In fact, ever since you were shot, he hasn't been able to take his eyes off you. Good thing he didn't know you were ready to walk away from fieldwork before Dad had to retire. He'd never let you forget that and he'd find a way to use that knowledge to his advantage."

"I know. Enough of this already," Francine said as she stood and picked up her electronic tablet. "You did look over the case file, right?"

"Yep. I wonder what made Tiffany switch agencies anyway." Farrah raised herself up off the sofa.

"Who cares?" Francine said.

"I do. It could be a factor in what we have to do for them." Farrah placed her right hand on her hip.

"No...you're just nosey," Francine said.

"All right...that, too," she agreed reluctantly. "By the way, have you started working on Felicia's storage chest yet?"

"No, why?"

"I loved the sketch of it and I was hoping I could convince you to make me one, too," Farrah said, giving her that cheeky smile she often used when she wanted something.

Francine laughed and shook her head. "Time to get back to business. I see you took your hair down," Francine said, pointing at her sister's head.

"Yeah, Meeks thought we shouldn't confuse the client too much. Does Mr. Morgan know you're part of a set of triplets?" Farrah asked sarcastically.

Francine laughed, picked up her phone and headed for the conference room attached to her office. "No, but what man you know wouldn't want a couple of butt-kicking sisters in his life?"

Chapter 5

As expected, Bill Morgan's and Tiffany Tanner's eyes grew wide as the sisters entered the room. Francine smiled and extended her hand to their guests, who had risen from their seats. "Mr. Morgan. Tiffany. Nice to see you again. This is my sister and business partner, Farrah Blake. Farrah's our chief legal officer, and she ensures that your, as well as our, legal rights and responsibilities are well protected. And from time to time, as in this instance, we work together and act as case leads."

"Pleased to meet you," Farrah said as Mr. Morgan took the hand she offered and gave it a small shake.

"That's great news," Mr. Morgan said on a sigh.

"Oh, my," Tiffany said, flashing looks between the two women. "You're twins... Identical."

"Not quite identical, and we're actually two-thirds of a set of triplets. When we were born, our eyes were all the same shade of green. As we grew, the color changed. Now we all have different eye colors. Mine are blue," Farrah explained, fluttering her lashes. "Francine's stayed green, and our baby sister Felicia has hazel eyes."

"Wow. Does your other sister work here, too?" Tiffany asked as she took a seat at the end of the table closest to both the window and the door.

"No, she works in another industry. She's a doctor, actually," Francine said proudly. "I really don't think our clients could take all of us working here."

"Or our staff, for that matter," Farrah added.

"It must be nice to have two other people in the world that you can depend on no matter what," Tiffany said, sliding down farther into the chair, her wistful tone speaking more to the loneliness she felt at being an only child than any actual jealousy she had toward the sisters' relationship. The twenty-one-year-old beauty pulled out her cell phone and began tapping her index finger on the screen as though she was suddenly disinterested in what was happening around her.

Francine and Farrah gave each other a knowing glance.

"Please sit," Francine said to Mr. Morgan, who focused his blue-eyed gaze on his client. "This shouldn't take very long. I just have a few follow-up questions for you."

"No problem…whatever you need," Mr. Morgan replied, taking a seat next to Tiffany. "We're just happy you'll be handling this case yourself."

Bill Morgan had been a family friend and attorney to the Tanner family for years. He'd played a significant role in helping the Tanners nurture Tiffany's career. In fact, he'd become Tiffany's legal guardian and business manager after her parents were killed in a tragic boating accident when she was twelve. By all accounts, at the time, the recently divorced thirty-two-year-old had been an excellent father figure for the shell-shocked child and a stern guiding hand during those highly publicized and turbulent adolescent years. When Tiffany turned twenty-one, she took control of her career and gained access to a multimillion-dollar fortune that her parents had left her. By the looks of things, Tiffany and Mr. Morgan were still adjusting to their new relationship.

"I see Kelly has taken care of you already," Francine said, gesturing to the water and coffee that had been provided. "Would you like anything else? A refill?"

"No, thanks. We're fine," Mr. Morgan replied after checking with Tiffany, who signaled her disinterest with a wave of her hand.

Francine cracked open her tablet. "All right then, let's get started. We checked out—"

"I have to know," Farrah said with a quick glance that silenced Francine. "Why us? What made you decide to pick Blake & Montgomery to replace your old security firm?"

Mr. Morgan's jaw was clenched but relaxed before he answered. "According to our reports, you're *the* best firm in the country. Especially when it comes to dealing with personal security," he explained.

"As you know, Tiffany is the biggest celebrity client we've ever agreed to manage. While we've assisted other agencies with their celebrity client base, Tiffany will be the first we've agreed to handle exclusively."

"You've made that perfectly clear, and as I said before, your company's reputation in international security rivals no other. We're honored to be your first official celebrity client," he said with a slight nod and a curve of his lip.

"Then why didn't you come to us in the first place? It's not like you knew for sure we didn't cater to celebrities at that time. There's always an exception to every rule," Farrah asked.

"Farrah!" Francine warned.

"It's okay," Tiffany defended, waving off Francine's

concern with a flip of her diamond-studded hand and a wide smile. "The other company came highly recommended from a reputable source," she explained with a look at both Francine and Farrah.

"So why the change?" Farrah pressed.

"We thought it would be nice if there were more female agents around," Mr. Morgan said before Tiffany could answer.

"Female agents…what are we missing?" Farrah continued to question.

Mr. Morgan looked at Tiffany, who was putting her phone into her Prada bag. Before he could say anything, Tiffany sat up in her chair, pushed a wayward strand of blond hair behind her ear and said, "I have a stalker."

"Okay. Any firm can deal with that," Farrah said with a small frown and a slight tilt of her head.

"He was a part of my security detail," she added.

"We think he *might* have been a part of the security team," Mr. Morgan corrected. He was clearly not convinced, and he gave Tiffany's hand a small, condescending pat. "We don't know for sure."

"Why do you think that? I mean you've had the same team for two years, and they're all good men," she said, shaking her head. "We've checked them out."

Tiffany stood, walked to the window and stared out at downtown Houston. The room was quiet for several moments before she spoke.

"I found notes and gifts in my bedroom…in my underwear drawer. Every time I get a new phone number, my stalker seems to get it," Tiffany explained without facing the group. "The last straw was when I started receiving pictures of naked body parts in my personal email." She looked over her shoulder at Francine. "The only people who had access to my home and private numbers, other than my family and a few close friends, were the members of my security team."

"We'll need a list of those names—both family and friends," Francine said.

Tiffany turned and faced the group. "Why?" she asked, frowning.

"Because they'll need to be checked out," Farrah said. "*All* of them."

"Did you report this to the police?" Francine asked as she reached for her cell phone. While she waited for a response, she texted Meeks: Conference room. Now. And bring Robert.

"No," Mr. Morgan said, again looking at Tiffany as if taking direction from her as to how much he should share.

"Why the hell not?" Farrah asked through narrowed eyes.

"Farrah…" Francine said with a warning glance in her sister's direction.

Tiffany returned to her chair and took a long sip of her water.

Before she could reply, Meeks and Robert walked through the door. "Bill Morgan, Tiffany Tanner, this is our chief operations officer, Meeks Montgomery, and head of our corporate security division and resident computer expert, Robert Gold. He helped develop the systems we'll be installing in your home," Francine introduced.

After handshakes all around, Meeks and Robert took seats at the conference table.

"I asked them to join us because in a case like this," Francine said, looking around the table, "it's best to not only get the police involved, but to make sure all parties involved in your security are fully aware of the situation."

"What situation would that be exactly?" Meeks asked Francine with narrowed eyes.

Francine brought Meeks and Robert up to speed on the situation as they knew it, and as expected, Meeks took over the questioning.

"Stalkers aren't to be played with," he explained with a pointed look at Tiffany. "What makes you think it's someone from your former security team?"

Tiffany took another sip of water and said, "I had an affair with a couple of guys on my security team."

"A couple?" Robert asked, his eyes wide.

Both sisters glared at Robert. He shrugged and mouthed, "What?"

Mr. Morgan reached for Tiffany's hand and gave it a supportive squeeze before saying, "Tiffany, you don't have to—"

"Yes, she does," Meeks said. "We need to know everything if you want us to be able to protect her."

"It's okay, Bill," Tiffany said before removing her hand from his grip and taking another sip of her water. "I'm twenty-one years old, and I've been working in this industry for ten years. For the last four years I've had some exceptionally good luck, which required me to be even more selective with the people I associate with."

"Exceptionally good luck?" Robert said sarcastically as he too flipped through his electronic tablet. "You've had three back-to-back blockbuster movies and gained access to a fifty-million-dollar trust fund. Yeah, I'd say that's some exceptionally good luck."

Tiffany smiled. "I've never wanted to be one of those childhood stars that ended up broke and in the gutter somewhere, and my family and Bill made sure that would never happen."

Tiffany gave Bill a smile that clearly expressed gratitude, but his responding smile seemed to offer more than paternal love.

"Do you have any idea how hard it is to make friends? I mean, *real* friends?" she asked, her voice rising an octave. "Let alone trying to find a nice guy? Trust me, it's not easy. So I find myself gravitating toward my security team."

Tiffany got up and walked around the table and stared out the clear glass wall of windows that looked out over the city. She wrapped her arms around her body and slowly moved her hands up and down her arms. The room was at a comfortable temperature so Farrah recognized the gesture as a defense mechanism and asked, "Tiffany, would you like to take a break?"

Tiffany turned away from the windows and faced her. She wiped away a lone tear that had escaped her left eye and said, "No…I'm fine. What more do you need to know?"

"Is this really necessary?" Bill demanded as he made his way around the table to stand next to Tiffany, where he placed his arm around her.

"I'm afraid so," Francine said before she continued to question Tiffany about her relationships with members of her former security team, her friends and her normal routine—all under Meeks's heated scrutiny, which appeared to have made the air slowly evaporate from the room.

Another hour and several cups of coffee later, Tiffany had finally decided she'd had enough. "I'm exhausted, and I have an event tonight," she said, gathering her things. "So if you need any more information, feel free to join me at the house."

"I'll accompany Ms. Tanner home and get the team in place," Robert said as he too gathered his things to leave. "While I'm there, I'll figure out what updates her current security system may need."

Meeks nodded. "And we'll have any necessary adjustments made first thing in the morning."

"That's great. Robert and Farrah and I will accompany you to your event this evening until we can assign someone to watch over you on a more permanent basis," Francine explained to Tiffany.

Tiffany breathed a sigh of relief and said, "Thank you."

Francine could feel Meeks's eyes on her, but she ignored him and continued to go through her security checklist.

Meeks pulled out his cell phone and started dialing. "I'll contact a friend of mine at the police department—"

"Is that necessary?" Mr. Morgan questioned Meeks. "The way I understand it, you have better resources than most police departments across the country. Besides, we really don't want the press to get wind of any of this. Why can't you just handle this on your own?"

"You didn't let me finish," Meeks added. "I'll see if he's willing to make a house call and take the police report there. That way, there's less of a chance of this news getting out. There are protocols with everything we do, and while we will do everything in our power to find the person that's behind all this, our priority has to be to keep Tiffany..." he slid a glance at Francine, "and our team safe," Meeks told Mr. Morgan, leaving no question as to his priorities.

"Having the police work with us on finding Tiffany's stalker will hopefully make apprehending him that much easier," Francine offered. "And the sooner we can put that person behind bars, the sooner we can get Tiffany settled into that routine we discussed earlier," she reminded Mr. Morgan, who acknowledged her statement with a simple nod.

"Thanks, I'd appreciate that," Tiffany said, making her way to the door. "The less publicity this thing generates, the better."

"Farrah and Robert will see you out," Francine said.

Farrah gave her sister a small nod and said, "After you," to their guest.

Francine waited for the room to clear before she turned to pick up her tablet and found Meeks glaring at her. "What? Go ahead, say it. I'd hate for you to spontaneously combust from holding back," she declared as she retreated to her office, knowing that he would follow.

Chapter 6

"Are you crazy?" Meeks asked Francine as he followed her into her office. He closed the door behind him with enough force to make his point.

"Last time I checked I wasn't, but let me check again," Francine replied, tapping her index finger against her temple. "Nope…still not crazy."

Meeks walked around her desk to stand in front of her with his arms folded across his heaving chest. "Then why the hell do you insist on doing crazy shit?"

She raised her chin and crossed her arms, matching his stance before asking, "What are you talking about, Meeks?"

"What am I—" He took a deep breath. "I'm talking about you taking the lead on this stalker case—a case that has danger written all over it. Especially with what we know now, our experience and your dumb luck, it is likely someone who's familiar with our line of work! *That's* what I'm talking about," Meeks explained as he took another step closer to Francine.

Francine blew out a breath and rolled her eyes in exasperation. "Not this again."

Meeks took the final step forward that had them mere inches apart. She stared up into his eyes and dropped her hands to her sides. Meeks watched as her breathing escalated, as her breasts slowly rose and fell. He dropped his arms and fisted his hands at his sides to keep himself from reaching out to caress them. He could imagine the taste and the softness of them and grew hard. Francine held his gaze and bit down on her lower lip—another move that made things worse for him. The sexual tension in the air was like a fog circling around them.

After several moments of tense silence, Meeks couldn't resist any longer. He raised his right hand and traced the tip of a finger slowly across Francine's lower lip. The feel of her silk-like skin made his hand tremble slightly. He captured Francine's chin in between his thumb and index finger, raising it slightly as he slowly began to lower his head and held her gaze.

Francine rose up on her tiptoes and wet her lips. The sight of Francine's pink tongue nearly sent Meeks over the edge, and he leaned in to capture her mouth.

Knock, knock.

Farrah, as usual, had entered the office before being invited in. She stood smiling in the doorway and asked, "Excuse me…am I interrupting something?"

Francine and Meeks continued to stare at each other for several additional seconds before Meeks dropped his hand, straightened to his full height and said, "No…not at all." Meeks gave both women a curt nod before making his exit.

When Meeks returned to his office, he closed his door and proceeded to bang his fist against it. "Shit! What the hell is wrong with you?" he asked himself, rubbing his knuckles. "Okay, so she looks exceptionally beautiful when she's angry," he mused aloud. "So what if she was just as turned on as you were? You know better. You could have made a big mistake."

"You usually bang your fist against the door and talk to yourself? And who looked exceptionally beautiful?" a soft voice asked from behind him.

A wide smile spread across Meeks's face before he turned around. "Hello, Mother," he said as he walked forward and into his mother's extended arms. "What brings you into the city? Did I miss an appointment?" Meeks kissed Constance Montgomery on both cheeks.

"How sad is that? A mother has to make an appointment to visit her own son," Constance said, holding him at arm's length. It was clear where Meeks had inherited his tall frame, fair skin and dark brown eyes.

Mother to Meeks and his younger brother Matthew, Constance had been a fixture at Blake & Montgomery when her husband was the company's COO. Milton Montgomery joined his best friend and former army ranger buddy Frank Blake in his desire to build a corporate and personal protection security firm that rivaled no other. Together, they had worked hard for years, using their extensive military combat and weapons training and worldwide contacts to do just that.

While Constance never played an active role in the business, the stay-at-home mom made sure her family spent as much quality time together as possible, even if that meant piling the boys into the car and driving to the office to spend that time with their father. The boys had loved the on-site gym in particular, but more important, they loved family togetherness.

"Don't start, Mother," he teased, taking the hat and jacket she offered and placing them on his desk. "Scheduling times for visits was your brilliant idea, remember? You know you can drop by and see me whenever you like."

She shook her head, the movement causing her stylish gray bob to release itself from behind her ears and frame her round face. "Yeah, right. And take a chance on you being out on some assignment? No, thank you."

Meeks gave her a toothy grin. "So…what did I do to deserve this unexpected pleasure?"

"Better," Constance said as she released her grip on her son and sat her tall frame eloquently into the chair facing Meeks's desk.

Meeks followed suit and settled into the chair next to her.

"I came to town for my monthly lunch with Mary and Victoria," she explained, crossing her legs at her ankles. "Victoria is meeting us at the restaurant, and since I was a little early to pick up Mary, I thought I'd stop in and say hello to one of my two favorite sons," she explained as she fluffed out her hair.

"Well, that's—"

"But enough of that," she said, ignoring his attempt to respond. "Tell me why you were banging your fist against the door." Constance clasped her hands and placed them in her lap. "And who's incredibly beautiful when she's angry, as if I don't already know, and why was she angry?"

"Mother, I don't—"

Constance held up her hand to stop his protest. "You might as well tell me, because you know I'll get it out of you eventually. Is this about Francine?"

Meeks took a deep breath and sat up straighter in his chair. "It's not that big of a deal. Francine and I had a slight disagreement about a business situation and that's all there is to it."

"You usually bang your fist against the door after a

business disagreement?" Constance asked her son with questioning eyes.

"Really, Mother, there's nothing for you to worry about," Meeks said as he reached for Constance's hand and gave it a reassuring squeeze.

"You know, Victoria tells me Francine is still single."

Please don't go there, Mother. Not today. "If she doesn't stay out of trouble, she'll stay that way," he murmured to himself.

"What was that, dear?" his mother asked. She gave him a knowing smile, the kind that she'd often given when he and his brother were growing up.

"Nothing," he mumbled. "I just know where this conversation is going, and as I've told you a thousand times, Francine and I can never have a relationship."

"You've been in love with that woman for most of her life. I understood and agreed with your decision to stay in that friend and protector lane when she was younger. But son, Francine is a grown woman now and something special has grown between you two through the years. That big brother, protective seed sprouted into something wonderful and if you let it, it could become something magnificent."

"Mother, I know you mean well. I just can't. We're too different."

Constance released a deep slow sigh. It was a gesture that told Meeks to shut up and listen, which he did. "Son, I love you, but sometimes you're too much like your father, God bless his beautiful, stubborn soul. You know better than most just how short life can be, but living in fear of loving someone isn't the answer," she said, twisting her wedding band on her finger. "Can you honestly tell me that you have no feelings for Francine?"

"Meeks, man, I need you to take a look at this…" Robert said, walking into Meeks's office without knocking or looking up from his tablet. As he saw Constance, he added, "Oh, excuse me. No one was out front and I didn't realize you weren't alone."

Constance turned slightly in her chair and smiled up at Robert. "He's not, and you better get over here and give me a hug, young man."

Robert offered her a wide smile. "Yes, ma'am." Robert took her hands, pulled her up from the chair and into a big hug. "You look beautiful, as always."

"And you're a charmer, as usual," she said, kissing him on both cheeks. "How's your mother? I've been meaning to call her."

"She's doing great, and I know she'd love to hear from you."

Constance smiled and gave Robert a small pat on his cheek. Meeks shook his head at the sight, feeling grateful for the interruption. "What's up?"

"Just a slight scheduling issue, but it can wait," Robert declared as he started backing up, easing closer to the door.

"Wait one second, mister." Constance collected her hat and coat from Meeks's desk. "You two have business to tend to, and I have a lunch to get to. Besides, I'm sure my son is grateful for the subject change."

Robert cut his eyes to Meeks, but remained still and silent.

"Mother, I…" Meeks said before falling silent. He stood and stared at her like a child searching for an excuse for doing something wrong. But in his case, it was the right answer to her question.

Constance smiled. "That's what I thought."

"I'll walk you out," Meeks offered.

"Don't be ridiculous. I can find my own way out. Besides, you two have work to do, not to mention you have some serious thinking to do, too, young man," she said, leveling her son with a poignant look.

Meeks helped her into her jacket.

"You know, Francine's nothing like that redheaded girl you dated there for a while. I never really liked her."

Robert burst out laughing.

"Yes, Mother, I know," Meeks said, giving Robert the evil eye as he walked her to the door.

Constance embraced Meeks, then kissed both him and Robert gently on the cheek and left his office.

"So what was that all about?" Robert asked.

"Nothing," Meeks said, walking back to his desk. "What's the problem with the schedule?"

"Oh no, you don't." Robert sat in the seat vacated by Constance. "What were you trying to avoid with your mother?"

Meeks sighed and moved to stand in front of his window. He stared out at the Houston city skyline for several moments before he responded. "My mother thinks I should talk to Francine about these unresolved feelings she believes we have for each other. It doesn't seem to matter that we want different things."

"Let me guess, you don't think you *have* unresolved feelings for each other," Robert said in a sarcastic tone.

"No, it's perfectly clear how we feel about each other, and neither one of us thinks it's necessary to explore them any further."

Robert tilted his head slightly. "You do know how ridiculous you sound right now, right? How do you know what Francine wants and doesn't want if you haven't talked to her about it? According to our mothers, relationships are about compromise...on both sides."

"I know that," Meeks said, trying to keep the frustration from edging into his voice. "But when it comes to

Francine's safety, there is no compromise. She seems to want to play superhero these days," Meeks said with a little more force than he intended.

Thoughts of Francine in the hospital, looking weary and helpless, flashed through his mind. Those images tightened his gut with worry. And now she was putting herself back on the hook, and he knew it was because she was trying to prove a point—to him. He felt himself beginning to lose control, and he needed a moment to bring his emotions back in check.

"Francine is obviously smarter than you're giving her credit for. Do you think she'd intentionally put herself in danger?"

Meeks turned to face his friend. "Maybe not intentionally," he said, his voice barely above a whisper. "Remember when she got shot?"

"Do I? I thought you were going to kill everyone in the hospital when they tried to stop you from seeing her." Robert smirked.

Meeks nodded his head slowly. He couldn't remember how many laws he broke just driving to the hospital. "I wanted to," he replied.

"I bet," Robert said.

Meeks turned back to face the window. "I wasn't with her that day. I couldn't protect her. I really don't know what I would have done if I…if I'd lost her."

Robert pushed out a breath as he ran his right hand through his hair. "I get that. But no matter how careful we are, there are some things we can't control, like our feelings."

Meeks returned to his desk. "I just—"

Robert stood and leveled his sights on his friend. "Just talk to her, man."

No matter how great the attraction or potential for a future there could be, having a woman…a wife…in constant danger wasn't an option. Regardless to how hard it was going to be, Meeks knew he had to keep things between him and Francine professional.

Chapter 7

Francine looked at her sister's smiling face and put up her hand to stop the verbal barrage she knew was coming. "Don't say one word. Nothing happened." Francine returned to her desk and haphazardly began to move papers around.

"I wasn't going to say a thing," Farrah said as she entered the office and took the seat in front of her sister's desk.

"I mean…he started to kiss me," she continued. "At least, I think he was going to kiss me."

Farrah's eyebrow shot up. "You *think*? If you don't know, it really has been too long."

"Anyway, it doesn't matter. It didn't happen, and it's not going to." Francine sat down, put her head in her hands and shook it.

"Are you upset about what *almost* happened or what didn't happen?" Farrah questioned.

Francine gave her a noncommittal shrug.

"Look at me, Francine," Farrah commanded.

Francine raised her head and slowly dropped her hands to her desk, giving her baby sister her undivided attention.

"Do you remember that summer when we were six and Meeks was thirteen? It was the first summer we spent with him and Matt at the beach house."

"Of course I do," she said, smiling at the memory.

"Do you remember how we tried to play tricks on them by switching our identity? Our eyes were still basically the same color, so besides Mom, Dad and Mary, no one could tell us apart."

"No one but Meeks," Francine offered.

"No, he could always tell *you* apart from me and Felicia. No matter what we did," Farrah said, crossing her arms. "It was like you two were connected or something. We tried to trick him every summer until we were eleven, the summer before he left for college."

Francine smiled. "He did always know which one was me, didn't he?" she murmured to herself.

"Remember our eighteenth birthday party?" Farrah asked with a raised eyebrow. "Meeks spent most of the night staring at you and giving warning glares to anyone that danced too long or close to you."

Both sisters laughed. "Yeah, it took me forever to realize why no one wanted to slow dance with me. Not even little Jimmy Taylor, who was fifteen and barely reached my shoulders, would accept my offer."

"And do I need to remind you of what a disaster our twenty-first birthday bash turned out to be because of Meeks? He'd convinced Dad we needed extra security there since we'd gained access to our trust funds," Farrah asked.

"As much as I've enjoyed this little walk down memory lane, what's your point?"

Farrah leaned forward. "My point is, the man has loved you forever, even if he didn't know it. If you're honest with yourself, I think you've loved him just as long. You should try talking this out with Meeks. I want you to be happy," she advised.

"But what if…" Francine shook her head.

"If what?" Farrah asked, frowning.

"I don't deny that for a long time there's been this crazy attraction or something going on between us—"

"Crazy attraction or something!" Farrah said, laughing. "The chemistry between you two could light up downtown."

"But what if that's all this is? Even if we could find a way to put our business differences aside, what if this thing turns out to be a phase and we ruin things between us?"

"But what if it turns out to be something wonderful? You can't keep avoiding your feelings."

Francine sat up straighter and took a deep breath. "I really appreciate what you're trying to do and I promise it won't affect the business. We're both professionals, and we won't let a little sexual tension get in the way of getting the job done." She shifted some papers on the desk. "I've seen a few of the women he's dated and I'm not his type. I'm happy with my life just the way it is."

"Whatever you say," Farrah said, her expression doubtful as she got up from the chair and headed to the door. "We have an event to get ready for, so unless you've changed your mind about taking point…"

"I've done no such thing." Francine picked up her briefcase, placed it on her desk and began placing files into it. "I'll meet you in the lobby, and we can head over to Tiffany's place together."

"Fine, just think about what I've said. Communicating with someone doesn't always have to be verbal. A gesture here, a look there, just might do the trick. You know how observant Meeks is, especially when it comes to you. It's time to light a match to that long fuse you two have been hanging on to for so long. Keep in mind that Tiffany's hosting an after party for the media, cast members and a few of her friends after the movie preview," she said, opening the door. "So be sure to dress for the occasion."

"Speaking of chemistry and fuses, what's going on with you and Robert? Things seem…different between you two," Francine asked, her face marred in confusion.

"Now that's a conversation for another time," she said as she left her sister's office.

Francine shook her head as she reached for her ringing phone and smiled. "Hi, Daddy."

Frank Blake, the girls' father and current chairman of the board of Blake & Montgomery, was on the line. "Hello, sweetheart, got a minute?"

"Of course."

"I wanted to talk to you about the next board meeting."

"Dad, I can't do this with you right now," she said, shaking her head.

He laughed. "You said you had a minute, and that was barely three seconds ago."

Francine sighed and sat on the edge of her desk. "All right…go ahead."

"Look, sweetheart, now that you've taken on this Tiffany woman as a client, you're going to have to be prepared to convince the board why you think handling clients of that magnitude is right for us. Otherwise, she could very well be our first and last superstar patron."

Francine took a deep breath and released it slowly before she spoke. "Dad, we've gone over this a million times already. Expanding our personal security business to include celebrities was the next logical step in our company's growth and as CEO of our company, it's my duty to look toward our future."

"I realize that, but the risk to everyone's safety, especially yours, just seems too great. Not to mention all the unwanted attention that comes with dealing with celebrities. As chairman of the board, it's my job to ensure that whatever direction you want to take the organization is what's best for us all."

"This isn't getting us anywhere, and I've got to go."

"All right, but just so you know, at next quarter's board meeting, I'll be bringing the celebrity protection line of business up for review, and if I'm not happy with what I hear, I'll call for a vote to eliminate it. And sweetheart, I'll have the votes," he said.

Francine knew that that was a real possibility. With the way the stock had been divided and the current split decision over the celebrity issue, it would be up to the board to decide which direction the company went. The way it stood now, her dad had all the votes he needed.

"I wouldn't count those chickens just yet, Dad," Francine said with as much confidence as she could muster.

"I'll keep that in mind," he said, laughing.

Her father's robust laugh always made her smile, even when she felt like crying. Francine could imagine his two-hundred-pound, six-foot body shaking as he laughed while running a hand through his curly black hair.

"Goodbye, sweetheart. I love you. Please be careful," he said.

"Goodbye, Dad. I love you, too. Tell Mom I love her."

"Will do."

Francine disconnected the call and placed her phone on the desk. She stood and picked up the file she'd removed

earlier from her wall safe labeled Board of Directors—
Top Secret and smiled. "No, Dad, I wouldn't count those
chickens just yet," she repeated to herself.

Chapter 8

Francine looked up from the document she held when a knock on the door drew her attention.

Kelly stood in the doorway waiting for permission to enter. "Excuse me, Ms. Blake."

"Yes, Kelly, what can I do for you?" Francine replied, sliding the papers into her briefcase.

"I apologize for the interruption, but your sister asked me to give you a message that she told me to read to you word for word." Kelly unfolded the pink piece of paper she was holding and recited, "Cine, I've decided to head over to Tiffany's place early with Robert so we can meet up with Danny. I want to get the lay of the land, as well as get the field portion of my assessment over with. I left you a voice mail message, but I figured you'd be too busy to check…"

Francine grimaced and picked up her phone and saw that she had in fact missed a call from both of her sisters, as well as from several clients.

"…and wouldn't get it until it was too late, hence the need for Kelly to read it to you. See you at Tiffany's later."

Kelly released a breath and held the message toward Francine.

"Thank you, Kelly. If there's nothing else?" she said, taking the message and placing it on her desk.

"No, ma'am," she quickly replied.

"Well, you can go and have a nice evening."

"Thanks, and you, too, Ms. Blake," Kelly said as she slowly walked backward out of the office.

Francine dropped her phone into the case that was attached to her hip and returned to the task of powering down her computer when there was another knock on her office door. This time she didn't bother looking up. "Forget something, Kelly?"

"It's not Kelly, and I don't forget anything," the voice replied.

Francine's body stilled, but all her female senses went on high alert. With that almost-kiss lingering in her thoughts, her body's response was almost immediate.

"Meeks," Francine whispered.

"Yes…it's Meeks," he said. He leaned against the doorway and stared at her.

Francine straightened and gave him a brief glance, while trying not to give him too big of a smile. "Sorry, I thought Kelly had come back," she explained as she continued to pack up her briefcase, no longer paying attention to what she was actually taking.

"So I gathered," Meeks said, placing his hands in his pockets. "You taking your stapler home?"

"Yes, as a matter of fact I am," Francine said, placing her right hand on her hip. "What can I do for you?"

Meeks grinned. "I won't keep you, but since we're the security detail and we're walking the red carpet together, I wanted to know if you would like to ride over to Tiffany's place together. I'll drive."

"Of course you will," Francine murmured.

"Excuse me?" Meeks said.

"Nothing. *You're* walking the red carpet?" Francine asked, closing and locking her briefcase. "You usually leave those things to one of the senior agents on the cases you work." She was finally ready to go but made no move to leave.

"Yeah, well…this case is different. You have a problem with that?" he asked, continuing to stand in the doorway, which was a rare move for Meeks, who always made himself at home in her office whenever he stopped by.

Stop stalling, she chided herself. *He's obviously back to treating you like a colleague, which is what you wanted… isn't it? Answer the man.*

"No… I have no problem with that at all."

"Good, then I'll meet you in the lobby in an hour." He gestured to the bank of elevators. "If you're ready, I'll go upstairs with you," he offered.

"Such a gentleman," she teased. Meeks was only offering to accompany her to the floor where their apartments were located to be polite, since safety was the least of their worries in their building. If she didn't accept, he would know that she was unnerved by his demeanor.

They rode up the four flights in silence. Within steps, Meeks was at his door and after a brief pause, he said, "See you at seven," and began to unlock his door.

Francine watched Meeks disappear behind his door and continued on to her apartment.

After letting herself into her place and securing the locks, Francine made her way to the kitchen, where she retrieved a bottle of Pinot Grigio from her refrigerator and poured herself half a glass. Francine usually didn't drink when she worked, but she needed to calm her frayed nerves if she was going to get through the evening, especially since Meeks would be in a tux. The guns and knives he carried as accessories only added to his sexiness.

Francine took her glass with her into her bedroom. She turned the knobs on the wall as soon as she entered the room, lowering the sheer screen that covered her floor-to-ceiling windows, quickly illuminating the bedroom. Francine took another sip of her wine as she placed her things on her dresser, then turned and smiled at the intricately designed oversize three-dimensional hand-carved maple wood headboard for her king-size bed. It was a masterful piece of art—Francine's personal design—that had taken two years to complete and was clearly the focal point of the room. Francine took a deep breath and slowly released it before saying, "Exquisite."

Francine always seemed to find her place of calm whenever she entered her bedroom. Her ability to create such pieces of art was something she rarely shared with others. This had always been her outlet for stressful situations, from her heavy class loads in school to having to prove she was more than a pretty face with a lot of hair in her male-dominated career choice. The few people who had seen her creations never understood what she got out of working so hard at creating something so wonderful, then refusing to share it openly with others. While all of her designs had been beautiful and unique, this particular piece caught those who saw it off guard. Her sisters just thought she had a big tree growing out of her wall, and its rough texture against the wintergreen paint supported their theory.

Francine's phone started dancing around her dresser. She picked it up and smiled as she read the screen.

"What are you doing calling me from your honeymoon?" Francine asked in a high-pitched voice that surprised even her.

"Girl, I finally came up for air. Married life is exhausting in a crazy, 'I can't get him naked fast enough' kind of way," a voice said, laughing.

"TMI, Paul... TMI," Francine said, chuckling.

Paul White was Francine and Farrah's stylist, personal assistant and best friend. They'd met Paul in high school and in spite of the fact that he had been two years younger than they were and painfully shy, they all clicked immediately. Throughout high school, the girls had been very protective of Paul, and that still held true today. The Blake girls had always wanted a little brother, and Paul fit the bill perfectly.

"Look, girl, I just want to remind you not to miss your hair appointment next week. I had to pull a lot of strings to get you in. This new location is extremely popular, so don't be late either," Paul said, laughing.

"Really...where's John? Shouldn't you two be doing whatever it is married people do when they're not going at it like rabbits on their honeymoon?" she asked, lying across her bed and using her hand to hold up her head.

"He's taking a nap, and if you listen to me, you can find out firsthand what married people do when we're 'not going at it like rabbits,' as you say. Speaking of which, what's new on the Meeks front?" he asked.

"Nothing!"

"Nothing? That's not what I hear," he said.

"Oh yeah, what exactly do you hear?" Francine sat up cross-legged in the middle of her bed, reaching for her pencils and sketchpad, smiling at the sketch of a wood chest she was going to make for her baby sister—who was currently working out of the country—as a welcome-home gift.

"I hear you took on a celebrity personal protection case, and he's not happy about it."

"To say the least. Wait, how did you know that? This case didn't come up until after you left for Europe."

"I have my sources," he said, using what he called his Deep Throat voice, which he used only when he was teasing her and her sisters.

"You're so silly," Francine said, giggling. "Look, you have a honeymoon to get back to, and I have an event to get ready for."

"Event? What event?" Paul asked excitedly.

"So your sources aren't that great after all, I see," Francine said.

"Whatever. Where are you going and more importantly, what are you wearing? I can't have you going out looking all *crazy*."

Francine rolled her eyes. "I realize my brilliant stylist is on his honeymoon, but I got this. And if you must know, it's a movie premiere and party."

"You sure? We can use FaceTime and I can help you pick something out. I helped Felicia out in the same way," Paul offered.

"You did? When?" she asked.

"Just before the wedding."

"Oh…well, thanks for the offer, but I'll be just fine," Francine said.

"Well, have fun. I have to go…my husband's waking up." Paul laughed. "I love calling him that. Love you, girl. See you in a few weeks."

"Love you, too," Francine said, tossing her sketchpad to the other side of her bed, getting up and walking over to her dresser.

Francine picked up her glass and entered her huge walk-in closet. It contained wall-to-wall built-in shelves. A marble-top island with tons of storage space sat in the middle of the room; a vanity sat to the left of the entrance, with an oriental chaise to the right. Francine stood in the middle of her closet, trying to decide what would be appropriate to wear.

Just as Francine finished off the last of her wine, she spotted the long garment bag that still hung from the back of the closet door. The dress had been given to Francine by a former client, a high-profile designer, as a personal thank-you gift. It had just been delivered a couple of days earlier, and she hadn't gotten around to putting it away.

Francine removed the dress from the bag, and a wide, mischievous smile spread across her face. She walked over to her full-length mirror, pressed the dress against her body and turned from side to side. Her sister's words came to mind. *What if it turns out to be something wonderful*? Francine laughed. "This dress is perfect. Appropriate enough for the event but enough to drive Meeks crazy, maybe even light a fuse," she said to her reflection. "Excellent!"

Chapter 9

As Meeks prepared for the evening's event, he did as his mother suggested. He thought about Francine and tried to remind himself of all the reasons why a relationship between the two of them was a bad idea. The danger and his fear of losing Francine in such a way were real and ever-present in his mind. The day that Francine was shot had been the catalyst that changed the dynamic of their relationship forever. Meeks's mind quickly traveled back in time several months to when he'd received Robert's call.

"*Meeks, you still in Galveston?*" Robert asked.

"*Yeah, why?*"

"*You driving?*" Robert questioned.

"*No...not yet, why?*" he asked as he walked to his truck. *Meeks knew something was off about Robert's tone.*

"*Good. Look, try to stay calm. Raymond Daniels made bail—*"

"*What! Daniels made bail? When?*" he demanded.

"*A few hours ago, but let me finish. Somehow he found*

out where Francine was, and he went after her. He shot her."

Meeks felt like he'd just been shot himself. He couldn't make his lungs work, and his knees buckled. Meeks gripped his truck's bed for support.

"Meeks, did you hear me? Francine's been shot."

"Yeah, I heard you," he murmured. "Is she..."

"Yes, she's alive. She's being taken to Ben Taub now," Robert reassured.

"She's alive," Meeks whispered.

"Yes, Francine's alive," Robert echoed.

Meeks pushed out a breath and said, "I'm on my way."

Meeks had made it to the hospital in record time after breaking every speeding law known to man. As Meeks stood at the door to Francine's hospital room, his hand shaking as he grabbed the door's handle, he knew his very survival depended entirely on Francine's.

"Francine, you're a very lucky woman," the doctor was explaining as Meeks walked into the room.

The doctor turned to meet Meeks's gaze as he fully entered Francine's hospital room. "If you'll wait outside for a moment, sir, while I'm speaking to Ms. Blake, I'll call you back in when we're done."

Ignoring the doctor's words, Meeks went and stood next to Francine's bed, giving her a half smile and the doctor a "make me" stare.

Francine rolled her eyes. "Dr. Jackson, this is Meeks Montgomery. He's a friend. It's all right. Please continue," she said.

Meeks knew Francine was probably furious with him for interfering but he knew she wouldn't show it in front of the doctor.

"As I was saying, the bullet entered the left side of your

body, damaging the splenic capsule and a couple of ribs before exiting—"

"Splenic what?" Meeks asked, his brows pulled together.

"It's a layer of tissue that entirely covers the spleen in a capsule-like fashion to protect it from direct injury," Dr. Jackson explained to them both.

"Sounds like she was very lucky," Meeks said.

"Very. We're fortunate that the bullet completely missed your spleen and we were able to make the necessary repairs without complications," Dr. Jackson told Francine.

Francine nodded her head slowly and looked up at Meeks, but he fought hard to keep his face expressionless.

"Thanks, Dr. Jackson. I appreciate everything you and your team did for me," Francine said, her voice barely above a whisper.

"No need to thank me. Just follow all the instructions that my nurse will go over with you in a few minutes. Number one on that list, get plenty of rest and don't overdo it."

As he remembered, Meeks's hands were clenched at his sides and his heart raced as he shook his head, trying to erase the memories as though they were a child's Etch A Sketch game. As Meeks began to calm himself, flashes came to him, from their childhood when he'd watched over Francine and her sisters in a way that a big brother would, to the moment he'd become the twenty-five-year-old fierce protector in love with an eighteen-year-old Francine, a young woman he knew he had to distance himself from.

As the years passed, Meeks continued to struggle with his feelings for Francine. While the perceived cons of taking their relationship to the next level outweighed the pros, his heart ached and his body craved her. Although, in his mind, he knew that their work was a hurdle that neither one of them was sure they could overcome, he was done listening to his head. It was time to follow his heart.

Forty-five minutes later, Meeks was using his reflection in the glass door of their building's lobby to adjust his tie when he noticed a beautiful reflection staring back at him. Meeks felt as though someone had reached into his chest and squeezed his heart. Every masculine cell in his body was on fire. It was like a live wire had charged his blood. Meeks had never been more aware of a woman before. He was struck by the intensity of his need, which only cemented his earlier decision.

Francine was wearing a full-length, strapless dark red dress that sparkled like diamonds and accentuated her hourglass figure. Her delicate shoulders and the swell of her breasts called to every male instinct he had. Half of her hair was layered softly upon her head, while the rest fell down her back. A diamond cross necklace and diamond stud earrings set off the outfit perfectly. Meeks found her understated confidence extremely sexy.

Meeks slowly turned to face Francine, and his breath caught as their eyes met. "Damn," he said to himself, but loud enough for Francine to hear him.

Francine gripped her matching clutch tighter at her side and smiled. "Thanks, I think."

"You look beautiful," he said without breaking eye contact. "Breathtaking, in fact."

"Thanks...you're not so bad yourself," she said, walking toward him and rewarding him with a sexy smile. Francine stopped in front of Meeks and brushed a small piece of lint from his lapel, causing his heart to skip a beat. The sweet scent of vanilla coming from her body assaulted his senses, nearly knocked the wind right out of him. Meeks cradled Francine's face in the palms of his hands and stared into her beautiful, shocked eyes before slowly lowering his head and taking her lips into a sweet but passionate kiss. It took every bit of his willpower to pull himself back.

"Wow," Francine whispered, blinking rapidly.

"Sorry, I couldn't help myself," Meeks said, holding Francine's gaze before he slowly dropped his hands.

"Maybe you shouldn't help yourself more often," she said, smiling and biting the side of her lip.

Meeks returned her smile. "Ready?" he asked, taking her hand and placing it in the crook of his arm.

"Anytime you are," she answered. And for a moment, he believed she meant she, too, was ready for something more between the two of them.

Meeks escorted Francine to the waiting bulletproof SUV limo. "Shall we?" He gestured for her to enter the vehicle ahead of him. "I'm really glad I opted to let someone else drive us to Tiffany's. You know, in case I can't help myself again."

Francine noticed that the double-breasted black tux, crisp white shirt and black silk tie Meeks wore clung to him like a second skin. He looked every bit the sexy, rich and powerful man that he was…that he always had been. Even as a young boy, Meeks held himself as though the world rested on his growing shoulders and he was going to make sure nothing bad happened to it. Francine was struggling with the effect Meeks and that kiss were having on her body. She was fighting to control the sensations she was feeling; her nipples were hard as marbles and she was having trouble controlling her breathing as she throbbed at her core. The masculine scent of Meeks, mixed with his cologne, made the short ride to the other side of the city nearly unbearable for her. She spent the entire time fighting the desire to climb onto Meeks's lap and kiss him again until they were both out of breath.

They arrived at Tiffany's place in time to collect everyone for the premiere. Francine exited the limo so fast anyone would have thought her dress was on fire. As soon as she saw her sister enter the courtyard and start walking her way, she released an audible sigh of relief, giving a professional once-over to her environment, making note of the three-story white colonial mansion with the massive water fountain sitting in the middle of the courtyard. Francine knew now was not the time for her and Meeks to explore their feelings. Having Farrah as a buffer was exactly what Francine needed; one second longer alone in that limo and she would have embarrassed herself.

"Cine...my, my, you look hot," Farrah exclaimed.

Francine smiled and gave a slight nod. "Thanks. You look pretty hot yourself, sis." She admired the short shimmery gold dress that hit Farrah mid-thigh. Her hair was pulled off her shoulders in an intricate French twist; small crystal flower pins were sticking out of it.

"This old thing?" Farrah replied, turning her back toward her sister, showing off the dress's deep scoop in the back. "I've had it at least two months," she said, laughing.

"Nice dress, Farrah. You look great," Meeks said as he came to stand next to Francine.

"Nice? That dress is better than nice. She looks fabulous," Robert corrected, winking at Farrah and never taking his eyes off her face. "She looks...good enough to eat."

Farrah gave Robert a slow, suggestive smile. "You look hot, too. Love the tux," she said, leaving Francine and walking toward him. She stood in front of Robert, who was standing next to the steps that led to a massive front door. With her hands on her hips, she gave him a slow once-over with her eyes. "You look like a full course a woman could enjoy her damn self!"

Meeks shook his head. "Now that that's all cleared up,

shall we get to work? Where are we?" Meeks asked, flashing a look between Robert and Farrah.

"There you go, taking over again," Francine said, brushing a bead of sweat from her nose. Meeks's take-charge attitude was just the remedy she needed to bring her wayward body under control and put her mind back on business.

Both Robert and Farrah provided Meeks and Francine with an update. After receiving the assessment of the security system and reviewing the recommended changes from the team leads, Robert provided a breakdown of the staff assignments.

"The team's in place and ready to go, but there's been a small hitch." Robert said.

"A hitch?" Francine asked as she pulled her compact from her purse to powder her nose. "What kind of hitch?"

"It seems Tiffany's management team has its own security specialist that they want on the case, too," Robert explained.

"What?" Francine said as she put her compact away.

"In fact, they want their agent to act as point person."

Francine folded her arms over her breasts. "I assume you explained that that's not how we work."

"And that it's unacceptable," Meeks added.

"Yes, of course I did, but her production company insisted," Robert confirmed. "Once I found out who the agent was, I figured you wouldn't have a problem with it, and we could work around it," he said to Meeks.

Meeks's forehead creased. "How do you figure that?"

Before Robert had an opportunity to clarify his point, Tiffany appeared in the doorway with three of her friends. While their dresses varied in color and style, it was clear that they were making a statement: they were young, rich and beautiful.

As the four women made their way over to where they all stood waiting, Meeks spotted the tall redhead standing in the rear of the group. Her black dress was short, tight and very sexy—there was nothing understated about it.

The redhead approached the group, focusing all her attention on Meeks.

"Jasmine," Meeks murmured as he approached the woman with his hands partially raised.

A slow smile spread across the woman's beautiful face. "Meeks, darling, nice to see you again," she purred as she took his hands and pulled him into a hug. "It's been a minute."

Meeks's ex-girlfriend, Jasmine Black, a beautiful thirty-year-old redheaded Italian American he'd met at a security conference and dated for less than a year, had once told him how she'd been raised as the only child to a single father, a father whose inability to hold a job meant that there were times when she went to sleep hungry. As a child, Jasmine had vowed that once she grew up, she'd never go hungry again. Her ambition and resourcefulness helped her keep that pledge.

"Yes, it has. What are you doing here?" he asked as he dropped his hands and stepped out of her hold.

"They didn't tell you?" she asked, sweeping a gaze across everyone.

"I don't know what you're talking about," Meeks said, frowning. He turned and leveled a questioning stare at Robert and Farrah when Jasmine spoke up.

"I'm joining the team," she said, giving them all a winning smile.

Chapter 10

"Is she now?" Meeks asked, glancing quickly at Francine who said, "What?" at the very same moment.

Robert dropped his smile and took a step back. "It appears that the studio's production company is just as concerned as Mr. Morgan is about their star's well-being, and wants to have a hand in ensuring her safety," he said as he gestured for one of his men to see the ladies to the limo.

Tiffany and her friends moved toward the ride while Jasmine remained standing next to Meeks.

"When did they spring this surprise on us, and why am I just now hearing about it?" Francine asked Robert through narrowed eyes.

International security and investigations was a specialized field, with very few women working in the industry. It wasn't unusual for the women to have heard of one another's abilities and accomplishments even if they'd never met, and Francine knew exactly who the redheaded beauty was.

"We literally just got the call ten minutes before you arrived," Robert said defensively.

"Did you explain to them that personal security is a part of the service we're already providing?" Francine asked, taking a step toward Robert.

"You know we did, Cine," Farrah said, maneuvering so she stood between Francine and Robert. "The company insisted, and Mr. Morgan agreed, so Ms. Black's involvement isn't an option."

Francine silently glared at her sister for several moments. "Well, you should have—"

"You were almost here," Farrah explained, returning her stare full force.

Francine sighed. "So we really have no…"

Farrah waved her right hand. "It'll be fine."

"They're doing that twin-triplet communication thing again," Robert whispered to Meeks.

"I know. Freaky, isn't it?" Meeks said, causing Francine to focus on him for a moment before returning her attention to her sister.

"Very," Robert agreed. "Although…Farrah is sexy as hell when she's angry."

"Yeah, they both are," Meeks said.

"Twin-triplet communication thing?" Jasmine asked, her forehead creased.

"Yeah, they sometimes have these semiprivate conversations with each other. They aren't trying to be rude by leaving the rest of us out. Half the time, I don't even think they know they're doing it, and it just seems to happen," Robert explained as he watched the women's silent discussion continue.

"They've been doing that since they were kids," Meeks added.

Jasmine offered a quick nod and a wide smile. "Wow, that's pretty cool."

"By the way, how long have you worked for Tiffany and her management company?" Meeks asked, frowning. "Last I heard, you were doing the solo thing, strictly short-term contracts."

"Not long at all." Jasmine shrugged. "In fact, this is my first official gig for them and it's on a contract basis. I'm still doing my own thing. You know how much of a free spirit I am," she said, offering him a sexy smile.

"That I do," Meeks said. He could feel Francine's eyes on him the moment the words left his mouth.

"Cine, is it?" Jasmine asked no one in particular.

Francine turned from her sister to face Jasmine. "It's Francine," she corrected, offering her hand. "Francine Blake. Cine is an old family nickname. And you're J.B., right? I've heard a lot of great things about you."

Jasmine smiled, showing off a perfect set of white teeth and high cheekbones, then glanced at Meeks before returning her attention to Francine. "Yes," she said, accepting the extended hand. "Jasmine Black, actually. J.B. is a nickname, too. Pleased to meet you, Francine. I'm really looking forward to working with you."

Francine released her hand and gestured toward her sister. "This is my sister Farrah."

Farrah gave Jasmine a two-finger wave. Francine offered Jasmine a tight smile "Please don't take this personally, because you have a stellar reputation in the industry, but Bill never mentioned—"

"I'm sure we'll be able to work something out," Meeks interrupted, sending Cine a warning glance.

Francine bit her tongue and gave Meeks a short nod. "I'm sure we will."

"Time to get this party started," Tiffany yelled, sticking her head out the sunroof of the limo.

Meeks checked his watch. "Yes, we better go, or we'll make Miss Tanner late. I assume you're armed?" he asked Jasmine.

She extended her arms out at her sides and did a slow turn, giving Meeks a three-hundred-sixty-degree view. "Care to frisk me?" she asked, her tone every bit of husky.

"Jasmine…" Meeks sighed, keeping his gaze focused on her face.

Jasmine dropped her arms. "Of course I'm armed," she replied.

"Where?" Robert asked.

Farrah smacked Robert in the back of the head, and his smile disappeared.

"I'll ride with Tiffany," Jasmine said as she started making her way toward the limo. "Meeks, you coming?"

Francine moved forward. "Actually, I think I'll be accompanying Tiffany on the red carpet alone. Three of us on the carpet could be a bit much. That's all right, isn't it, Meeks *darling*?" she said over her shoulder.

"Right," Meeks replied dryly, as he followed behind both women.

Robert shook his head. He kept in step with Farrah as they headed for the area where the limos were parked. "This is going to be one long-ass night," Robert said to Farrah.

Meeks looked over his shoulder to give both of them the evil eye.

Everyone loaded into two black SUV limos—with two additional black SUVs following close behind—and made their way through the streets to the Theater District, a seventeen-block area in the heart of downtown Houston that was home to several premier entertainment complexes, including the Alley Theatre, where the premiere was being held. The two large searchlights, as well as the thousands of well-wishers that lined the street, made it impossible to miss the castle-like venue.

As they approached the theater, the screams of the thousands of people waiting behind the red velvet ropes to meet their favorite hometown actress were audible. As the group started exiting the vehicles, Meeks stopped Tiffany and her guests. He explained that he and Robert had to assure that their team was in place before allowing Tiffany and her entourage to exit the limo; the women reluctantly agreed. Farrah walked ahead of the group to ensure that everything in the lobby had been set up to their specifications. After the security experts were satisfied that everything and everyone was in place, Tiffany and her friends exited the limo.

Robert had another member of their team escort Tiffany's entourage through a separate side entrance, while Tiffany started ascending the massive red-carpeted steps leading to the theater's entrance. Jasmine walked alongside Tiffany but Francine brought up the rear. Tiffany and Jasmine laughed and smiled for the cameras as if they were lifelong friends, while Francine followed slowly behind them, keeping her eyes on the crowd.

"See anything out of the ordinary, anything out of place?" Farrah asked her sister through her earpiece.

"Other than Jasmine?" Francine replied dryly.

"Be nice, Cine," Farrah said.

"We're good," Francine responded.

"Ten-four. See you in a bit," Farrah replied.

The Alley Theatre, with its multiple towers and open-air terraces, had been commandeered and retrofitted for the movie premiere and after-party. The opulent decorations spoke to the period of the movie: the 1500s. The multilevel indoor reception area just outside the main stage where the movie would be viewed, bordering two elegant terraces that overlooked downtown Houston, showcased life-size pictures of Tiffany and the other cast members dressed in their costumes. Tiffany's latest movie was a period piece about Queen Elizabeth I.

The main stage, which accommodated seating for over eight hundred people, featured a massive viewing screen that had been erected for Tiffany's new movie. When everyone took their seats to watch the film, Meeks and Robert positioned themselves to secure the theater with half of their team, while Francine and Farrah secured the reception area with the other half. Once everyone was in their places, Francine walked out on the terrace.

"You all right?" Farrah asked as she exited onto the terrace behind her sister.

"Yes, of course," Francine replied, looking out over the city. Francine made a slight turn to face her sister and leaned against the cement railing. "Everything set for later?"

"Yep, everything's all good. Everyone's in place, and on the last sweep, the entire wait staff was briefed on when to start serving the food, and the champagne fountains have been set to start flowing right before everyone's scheduled to file out of the theater," Farrah shared, pushing a wayward strand of hair behind her ear.

"Good," Francine said with as much enthusiasm as she could muster. "I still can't believe how many people came out on a Tuesday night."

"This *is* Tiffany we're talking about."

Francine stood watching the lights of the city as she played with her diamond cross necklace—a nervous habit she'd tried hard to break, but under the circumstances, she decided not to beat herself up about it.

While Francine believed Tiffany's production company had only her best interests and safety in mind, she didn't buy that Jasmine's appearance was an innocent coincidence. What was worse was that Francine had no idea what Meeks thought about Jasmine's sudden appearance, and she was choking on her sudden bout of insecurity.

Farrah pulled her sister off to a quiet corner toward a set of counter-high tables and chairs, where they sat down. "Everything's set and we have several minutes to spare. So…you want to talk?"

"No," she snapped. "I don't want to talk about Jasmine or Meeks. And I certainly don't want to talk about Jasmine *and* Meeks."

"All right—"

"I mean, where *do* these people get off bringing in another agent without talking to us first? And why her? I know she's supposed to be good and all, but her, really?" Francine pulled out her compact and used the mirror to reapply her lipstick.

Francine knew she was being ridiculous but she didn't care. All she wanted to do was get through the night without hurting someone. At that point she wasn't sure who would be her first target: Meeks or Bill.

"So much for not talking about it," Farrah said. "Cine, it's not the first time a client has asked to have their own personal security assigned to their case."

"Yes, but not one where there's obvious history with one of the agents of record. Something's just not right about all this. Meeks's old lover showing up out of the blue like that can't be a simple coincidence. You know their breakup didn't end on the best note."

"Most breakups don't," she said, frowning.

"I just don't know why a woman with her credentials would take a job like this if she didn't have some ulterior motive."

"So this *is* about Meeks and Jasmine."

"Of course not," Francine said, grabbing a small bottle of water from the tray that had been placed in the middle of each table. "It's just we don't know anything personal about her," she said, staring down at the water bottle as if she'd forgotten that she was holding it.

Farrah smiled and shook her head.

"Other than the fact that she's tall, beautiful and has at least one creative way of hiding a weapon in a dress that fits like a second skin."

Farrah laughed. "We don't need to know anything personal about her. We know she's one of the best in the industry. In fact, she was trained by Meeks and they've even worked together on a few occasions since she went out on her own."

"I bet," Francine spit out, not even trying to hide her annoyance with the situation.

"Francine Blake, if I didn't know any better I'd say you were jealous."

"Don't be ridiculous." Francine took several sips of her water.

"Jasmine's no threat to you," Farrah said, grabbing a bottle of water for herself. "Everyone knows how much you and Meeks care about each other. We're just waiting for you two to figure it out and do something about it already."

"Farrah—"

"No, listen to me," she said, raising her voice slightly because a live band had started playing. "I know you're concerned about your lack of experience," Farrah said, interrupting a protest she knew was coming.

"I'm not—"

Farrah held up her hand. "Yes…you are. And it's not necessary. So what if the only two men you've been with were both jerks? We both know sex doesn't keep people together. It's everything else that goes on between you that does." Farrah took a sip of her water. "Besides, when you're as emotionally connected as you and Meeks are, there's no such thing as bad sex."

Francine shook her head. "I'm not doing this here," she snapped.

"Cine, this isn't like you. You really have to deal with this thing between you and Meeks," Farrah said with concern in her voice.

"Not tonight, I don't! Let's just get through the premiere without any incidents so we can call it a night," Francine said.

"You know, if you want to cut out now, you can. We have more than enough folks on hand to cover things here."

"Thanks… I'm fine," Francine said, never taking her eyes off the city's skyline.

Farrah sighed and fell silent.

The sisters sat in comfortable silence, periodically sharing idle chitchat while they waited for the movie to end. After an additional hour had passed, the theater door opened and everyone filed out and started mingling.

The sisters stood simultaneously. "Time to get back to work," Farrah said as they went and stood in the doorway that separated the reception area and the terrace. Francine stood back and reveled in the way her team successfully mingled in and out of the party guests, ensuring everyone's safety, especially that of their clients, seamlessly.

Francine's eyes scanned the room and landed on Jasmine, who was standing and laughing with Tiffany. Several men watched their interaction; they couldn't keep their eyes off the woman with flaming red hair, long legs and perfect butt. Her clear disinterest didn't seem to discourage them, either.

Farrah followed her sister's line of vision. "You got to give it to her. The woman has style," she said.

She has something, all right.

Francine watched as Jasmine made her way over to where Meeks was standing. The exaggerated way she swayed her hips sent a clear message to Meeks and everyone else watching—she wanted him. Francine could feel the jealousy she refused to acknowledge bubbling up inside her. *You're dangerously close to reaching your breaking point; it's time to call it a night.*

"Things are starting to wind down and you and Robert are here, not to mention Meeks and what's-her-name," Francine said, smirking.

Farrah's eyes grew wide and her lips parted slightly.

"Kidding, I was just kidding," Francine clarified. "I think I'm going to call it a night."

Farrah giggled. "No problem."

"Good night, sis." Francine gave Farrah a hug and made her departure virtually unnoticed.

Chapter 11

Francine entered her apartment, locked the door behind her and kicked off her shoes. She went to her refrigerator and removed the bottle of Chardonnay she'd pulled from her prized wine collection before she left. She took a glass from her cabinet and poured some for herself, which she polished off while standing in the middle of her kitchen. After refilling, she returned the bottle to the refrigerator and headed to her bedroom. But before she could make it down the hall, there was a knock on her door.

"Now what?" she murmured as she placed the glass on the bar and went to the door. Francine leaned forward and checked the door's peephole. *Seriously*? Meeks had his tie loosened and top button undone. She thought the man was too sexy for words.

Francine took a deep breath and exhaled slowly before she opened her door. "What are you doing here?"

Meeks's gaze lowered to her feet. "Nice polish," Meeks said, admiring her red toenails.

Francine wiggled her toes. "Thanks. What are you doing here?"

Meeks leaned into her doorjamb and gave her a sexy smile that made her heart stop for several seconds. "You left before we had a chance to talk. The party was wrapping up and as soon as Tiffany opens the last of her congratulatory gifts, the team will see her home. Besides, I think we've put this conversation off long enough."

Francine's body quickly moved through the stages of desire—from slow tingle to full-blown ache. She wasn't sure if the feelings were intensified by the wine or if it was all Meeks.

"Look, it's late," she said, gesturing toward the watch she wasn't wearing. "Whatever it is, can't it wait until tomorrow?"

"No, it can't. You going to let me in or what?" he asked, presenting her with another smile.

Francine stepped aside to let him pass.

Spotting her glass of wine on the bar, he asked, "May I join you?"

Francine retrieved a glass from the cabinet in the kitchen and the bottle from the refrigerator, then poured him a glass and handed it to him. An electric shock went through her body as their fingers touched.

"Have a seat."

Meeks took a seat at the bar while Francine leaned her hip against one of the bar stools. "What's so important that you had to come over now?"

Meeks drained his wine glass before he spoke. "Jasmine."

"What about her?" she asked as she took a sip of her wine.

"If she's going to be working with us, I thought we should talk about it," he said as he ran his fingers along the stem of his glass.

"More wine?" she offered, lifting the bottle on the counter between them.

"No, I'm good."

Francine replaced the bottle. "How much are you willing to share?"

"What do you mean?" Meeks pulled his tie free and placed it on the bar.

"Well, I know you've worked together, that you've even trained her. What I don't know is how personal your relationship got. It's obvious there *was* something between you two, right?"

"Right," he said as the line on his forehead deepened.

"Well, in all the years we've worked together, known each other, for that matter, you've never mentioned her... brought her around. I've at least seen the other women you've dated, but not her. What makes her so special?" Francine folded her arms under her breasts.

"Jasmine and I started working together before you even joined the company. I've probably worked with a lot of people you don't know, Cine."

"Don't do that. You wanted to talk, so let's talk. We both know that your relationship with Jasmine was more than professional. Was it serious and why hadn't we ever met her?" she asked before taking another sip of her wine.

Meeks pushed out a slow breath. "Jasmine and I dated off and on for a while, and by the time you'd joined the company, it was over. And in all the years that you've known me, have you ever actually met anyone that I may have been seeing?"

"No, I never actually met any of them. You either dragged them off so fast whenever I was around, or they were so enamored of you they didn't seem to even notice when other people come near. And why is that? You've certainly known about all the guys I've dated," she challenged.

"That's because your father had me checking them out and I've never dated anyone serious enough," he said, tilting his head with his left eyebrow raised.

"That's beside the point!"

"What is the point of your questions, Cine?" he asked, holding her gaze.

Francine shrugged. "I just want to make sure the professional and personal lines don't get blurred."

Meeks stood and closed the gap between them, trapping Francine against him and the bar. He removed the glass from her hand and placed it on the counter. Francine's breathing escalated, her breasts rising and falling.

"Are your questions professional or personal?" he asked, his eyes roaming from her heaving chest to her full lips, to stare into her eyes.

Francine's heart started racing, and her mouth suddenly went very dry as she leaned her head back in order to maintain eye contact. "Depends," she said, her voice barely above a whisper.

"On what, exactly?" Meeks whispered as he lowered his head, slowly rubbing his nose along her cheek before capturing her mouth, giving her a slow, gentle kiss that sent shock waves through her body.

The kiss turned deep and purposeful. His hands found her hair clip and released it, allowing her long locks to fall over his long fingers.

Francine was overwhelmed by his scent, his touch and his kiss.

Meeks raised his head slightly and gazed into Francine's desire-filled eyes. "I've wanted to do that all night," he said before taking her lips again. Meeks released her again but only long enough to add, "Truth be told, I've wanted to do that for years."

Right or wrong, Francine wanted him in this moment

more than she'd ever wanted anything in her life. Pushing aside all doubt and fear from her mind, she slid her arms up and around his neck. "Is that *all* you've wanted to do?" she asked, kissing the corner of his jaw.

"Hell no," he said, his voice deep and commanding. Meeks swept Francine off her feet. "And tonight's only the beginning."

Chapter 12

The beautifully lit Houston city skyline, blanketed by stars, pierced Francine's wall of windows and illuminated the bedroom. The setting was the perfect ambiance for what would prove to be a night to remember.

Meeks placed Francine on her feet next to her bed and began to kiss her along her jawline, her neck and her collarbone. "Breathe, Cine," Meeks reminded her on a soft laugh.

Francine released the breath she hadn't even realized she'd been holding.

Meeks took Francine's mouth again and again, leaving no doubt as to what would happen next. He pressed his forehead against hers. "We've been fighting this thing between us for years, and frankly, I don't have the strength or the will to fight it any longer. If you don't want this to go any further, Cine, you need to say so now...right now."

Meeks raised his head and gazed into Francine's eyes. He had made his decision as to how far he was prepared to take things with her; he was done denying what he wanted…needed. Now he had to give Francine the opportunity to come to that same conclusion, and he was praying that she would.

Francine tightened her arms around his neck and pressed her body against his. She kissed him under his chin and on the corner of his mouth. Francine ran her tongue over his lower lip, rose up on her tiptoes and pulled his face closer. She whispered in his ear, "Let me show you just how much I want this…how much I want *you*."

Meeks felt as though his heart was about to explode. It took everything in him not to take her where she stood but he knew she deserved better; they both did. He wanted to savor every single moment with her.

Meeks lowered the zipper on her dress and kissed the smooth skin underneath. She stood before him in a red lace strapless bra and panties, her dress pooling at her feet. Meeks fisted his hands to keep from reaching for her. He stood and enjoyed the view for several moments—the rise and fall of her breasts, the slight shiver she didn't even try to hide and the way she bit down on her lip. Meeks watched as Francine reached behind her back, unhooked her bra and let it fall to the floor. His eyes widened and his sex was hard as steel.

"My God, you're beautiful," Meeks said with a slight crack in his voice. "Cine…."

Francine smiled and reached for his shirt but before she could grab it, Meeks dropped to his knees before her.

"Oh…oh," Francine whispered.

Meeks kissed Francine down her stomach, along the top edge of her panties and down her hip. He reached up and cupped her breasts, running the pads of his thumbs over her nipples and squeezing gently. A soft moan escaped Francine's throat at the same time her eyes fluttered and closed.

Meeks slowly lowered Francine's panties, removing first one leg, then the other. He swung her left leg over his shoulders and ran his tongue and nose up and down her inner thigh, breathing in her scent. He dropped her leg and repeated the ritual with her right leg; only this time, Meeks's hands gripped her butt and he kissed Francine at her core. She threw her head back as her hips met each thrust of his tongue.

"Oh, Meeks...yes!" Francine screamed as she ran her hands through the fine hair on his head. Meeks used his teeth and tongue to send Francine over the edge, keeping his mouth on her until the tremors stopped.

Francine dropped her leg, collapsed back onto her bed and took several breaths. Meeks stood over her, giving her a wicked smile as he began to unbutton his shirt.

"Damn you. Two can play that game, you know," she said, smirking.

Francine propelled herself forward, unbuttoned his pants and lowered his zipper. Meeks's erection sprang proudly forward. Her smile faltered a bit. "My goodness... I'm not sure you'll fit," she said with a worried look on her face.

Meeks ran the back of his hand slowly down the side of Francine's face. "It's okay, baby...it'll be fine. Trust me."

Francine took him in her hands and began to gently massage his shaft, paying special attention to its tip. She leaned forward and brought him into her mouth, as much of his length as she could handle. Francine licked, sucked and pulled, closing her eyes as though she was lost in the moment. She found a rhythm that nearly brought Meeks to his knees.

Meeks pushed against Francine's shoulders and regretfully extracted himself from her mouth. "You keep that up and we'll be done before we get started."

Francine lay back on the bed and laughed.

Buzz… Buzz… Buzz.

Francine sat up on her elbows. "What in the world… who could that be?" she asked as she started to get up.

"No, you stay put," Meeks ordered as he grabbed his pants, putting them on as he made his way to the door.

Francine ignored the order and reached for his discarded shirt and followed him to the door.

Meeks opened the door to their nervous-looking doorman, Stan. "Sorry to bother you, sir, but Miss Farrah called—"

"Farrah, is everything all right? Did something happen?" Francine asked as she came up behind Meeks.

Of course she wouldn't stay put. Meeks glanced over his shoulder to find a bare-legged and barefoot Francine with her hair tousled about her head, wearing his shirt—a shirt that was barely buttoned and hanging off her like an oversize dress. Meeks's heart sped up and he gripped the door handle, quickly moving to block Stan's view.

"What's going on?" Meeks asked, turning his attention back to Stan.

"Miss Farrah's fine, but she tried to call…both of you. She told me to come to the door."

"What happened, Stan?" Meeks's frustration was clear.

"There seems to have been some type of incident at the theater."

"What kind of incident?" Francine asked as she reached for her cell phone.

"Sh…she didn't say. She only said that you should get back down there," Stan stammered.

"Thanks," Meeks said, sending the man on his way.

"Farrah, what the hell's going on?" Francine asked into her cell's speaker phone as she made her way back to her bedroom.

"Tiffany's stalker struck. She's fine, just a little shaken

up. I think you need to get back down here. You'll want to see this."

"We're on the way," Francine said, not thinking as she continued to change into their uniform.

"We…" Farrah said before Francine disconnected the call.

"I'll go change and meet you in the parking garage in ten minutes," Meeks said, heading for the door. "We'll take my Porsche."

"Of course we will," she said to his retreating back.

Within thirty minutes of speaking to Farrah, Meeks and Francine were once again pulling up to the Alley Theatre.

"I'll go find Robert and Farrah and see what's going on. You go find Tiffany. I'm sure she'll feel much better with you holding her hand," Meeks instructed as he exited the car.

"Like hell," Francine declared, following suit. "This is my case, Meeks. Remember? I'll find Farrah and Robert and only after I know what's happening will I go *comfort* Tiffany. Besides, you heard Farrah…she's fine."

Knowing Meeks would be on her heels, Francine turned and mounted the steps two at a time, spotting her sister in the lobby. "What's going on, and where's Tiffany?"

"I sent her home with Jasmine," Farrah explained.

"You what? Before I could make sure she was okay?"

Farrah gave a nonchalant wave. "Jasmine had everything under control," she replied.

The sisters started staring at each other but Robert quickly spoke up. "Now, now, you have to share with the rest of the class," he said, standing next to Farrah. "I know you're concerned but trust me, Tiffany's fine."

Francine held up her hands. "Okay, what happened?"

Farrah sighed. "Somehow Tiffany's stalker got past all

our defenses to leave her a very special gift. It was Jasmine who noticed something was out of place before we did, but not before Tiffany found herself opening an unwanted surprise."

"What was it?" Meeks asked, frowning.

"Follow me. You have to see for yourself." Robert led the group to a small storage room off the lobby.

"This room was empty and locked when we did our initial sweep," Farrah reassured.

Robert opened the door and switched on the light. Francine's eyes grew wide as saucers. A small round table stood with a clip lamp attached that was switched on, spotlighting several photos of both Tiffany and a man's—presumably the stalker's—private body parts spread across the table with a single black rose lying across it next to a propped card that read, "We'll be together soon."

Francine approached the table slowly. "Has the scene been processed yet?"

"Of course, our team took care of everything. We'll send the report to our contact over at the police department," Farrah said, handing her sister a pair of gloves. "I knew you'd both want to see this in person, so after they took pictures, videotaped and processed the room for prints, DNA and blood, I had them leave everything as is."

"Unbelievable," Francine said as she examined the photos.

"Tiffany got a text telling her she had another surprise waiting for her and she should go check it out alone."

"Did she recognize the name or number of the person texting?" Meeks asked as he circled the table so he too could examine the pictures.

"Nope, she just assumed it was all part of the celebration. Jasmine saw her go off on her own and she went after her, but she'd already opened the door before she could reach her," Farrah replied, shaking her head. "Tiffany fainted as soon as she saw the pictures."

"Poor thing," Francine said.

"Jasmine thought she saw someone that looked off, so she sent Nick after him while she secured the scene and made sure Tiffany was okay. As you can imagine, she was a mess," Robert advised.

Meeks's forehead creased. "Jasmine didn't give chase?"

"Nope, she took care of Tiffany and let our team handle it, just as she should have," Robert confirmed, giving him a knowing smile.

"And…" Francine's eyebrows stood at attention.

"And unfortunately we lost him in the crowd outside, but he dropped his hat. We'll process it. You never know." Robert gestured for a couple of their men to join them.

"Let's get this stuff back to the office so we can start examining it. See what it gives us." Meeks gave Robert a small nod, giving him the okay to have their men start packing up the evidence.

Francine noticed the exchange and rolled her eyes. "I should go check on Tiffany," Francine offered, hating how both turned on and frustrated Meeks could make her.

"That's really not necessary. Jasmine had the paramedics check her out before they left, and I called Dr. Perry and had him go by her place to make sure she's okay and give Tiffany a sedative so she'll be out for a while. Jasmine agreed to stay with her."

"Did she now?" Francine said, failing to hide the irritation she felt. She didn't understand why Jasmine doing her job aggravated her.

"Cut her some slack, Cine. She did great tonight," Farrah said, defending Jasmine.

"You're right," Francine admitted. "She really did prove

that she can be a team player. And having an extra set of eyes on this case isn't such a bad idea, after all."

The team spent the next several hours back at the office going over all the evidence they'd collected as they recapped the events of the evening before finishing for the night. Francine and Meeks stood close to each other as they rode up in the elevator in silence. The backs of their hands grazed before his pinky finger captured hers.

"My place is closer," Meeks said, reaching for her as the elevator doors opened.

Francine thought it was best if she and Meeks didn't try to recapture their missed opportunity...not tonight, anyway. No matter how badly she wanted him, she didn't want their first time together to feel artificial.

Francine stopped Meeks from reaching for his keys. "I think we should call it a night. It's late and we have an early day tomorrow."

Meeks slowly slid the back of his hand down the side of her face. "You sure about that?"

Francine laughed and her forehead fell to his chest. Her mind knew she was making the right decision, but her rebellious body had other ideas. Meeks sighed, wrapped his arms around her waist, kissed Francine on the temple and walked her to her door.

"Good night," Francine whispered before lowering his face down to hers for a kiss that made clear they had unfinished business.

Chapter 13

Francine walked into her kitchen, towel-drying her wet hair with her robe secured to her frame, to find Meeks standing there dressed in the company's uniform, pouring himself a cup of coffee.

"I see you let yourself in. You know, we all exchanged keys for emergency purposes," she said, heading for the coffeepot only to be handed a cup by Meeks.

"Good morning to you, too. French vanilla cream, just the way you like it," he said with the corner of his mouth curved up slightly.

"Good morning and thank you for the coffee," she said before taking a sip from her cup.

"Now as for my unexpected visit, I figured we should talk about what happened before things get too crazy today. Toast?" he asked, gifting her with that sexy smile she loved and handing her a couple of slices he'd just buttered.

"Thanks," she said, taking a bite.

"So, about last night," they chorused.

"You go ahead," Francine offered before taking another bite of her toast.

"How about we not have 'the talk'?" Meeks suggested, using air quotes to emphasize his point.

"What…why not?" she asked.

"Is it really necessary? I mean, we're adults and while last night was a unique experience for both of us, I'm sure we can find a way to get past it—"

"Oh, God!" Francine turned her back on Meeks and went to the living room and perched on the sofa.

Her heart sank. Had she imagined everything they'd said to each other? Everything they felt? Had she misinterpreted the whole experience? She fought back the tears that stung the backs of her eyes. Francine refused to give him the satisfaction of knowing he'd gotten to her.

"Wait…what?" Meeks asked as he followed her into the living room and kneeled down before her.

A lone tear that Francine could not hold back fell. "Baby, what is it? Why are you so upset?" he asked, a confused expression marring his handsome features.

"Don't call me that," Francine murmured, trying to turn her face away, only to have it held captive by his two large hands.

"Cine, please, what is it?" he begged, his eyes searching hers for answers.

"What is it? You just said you regretted what happened between us last night. Thank goodness we didn't take that final step," she said, desperately trying to hold the pieces of her heart together.

"I never said that," Meeks replied, dropping his hands to her arms, as though he'd just been shocked but somehow knew he couldn't break their connection.

"You did, you said you wanted to get past it…get past

last night," she said, angrily swiping away another wayward tear. "Like it was some….my God, what was I thinking?"

The thought of Meeks regretting what they'd shared—the words she'd secretly hoped and waited years to hear, the intimacy, things she had thought were just the beginning—was so painful that Francine was barely holding it together. She tried to extract herself from his hold, but he put a steel-like grip on her arms.

Meeks released a deep sigh and the corner of his mouth curved upward. He took Francine's face in the palms of his hands. "Cine, the only thing I regret about what happened between us last night is that we didn't get to finish what we started. I meant everything I said last night. I'm done fighting my feelings for you," he said before devouring her lips and kissing her passionately.

When Meeks finally let her up for air, she blinked several times to clear her vision. "But you said—"

"I was talking about Jasmine," Meeks said, anticipating her question.

"Jasmine," she said, frowning up at him.

"Yes, Jasmine being forced on us by Tiffany's management team, considering our history and all."

Francine had been so elated about the new developments between them—even if she had no idea where it was going—that she'd forgotten about everything else.

"Oh…that," she said as she wiped away a fresh set of tears.

"Yes…that," he said before giving her a kiss that left no doubt about how much he wanted her.

Francine sighed. "Just so I'm clear—last night was…?"

"Just the beginning. I know we have some differences that we need to work through, but I'm willing to give it a shot. That is…unless you feel differently than I do," he said, smirking.

Francine put her arms around his neck and kissed his nose and then his lips. "I think I can handle a beginning," she replied, smiling. "The rest, I'm sure we'll figure out."

"Good, let's talk more about this beginning of ours over dinner tonight. Oh, wait, I forgot it's the annual turnaround for the chemical plants—ten days of maintenance activities and quality checks. Thankfully, they only need us for a day and a half. Robert and I are taking off for Beaumont after lunch. We'll be back Thursday night, but I'm not sure how late I'll be. How about Friday night, my place at seven?"

"That works better for me, actually," she said. "I need to work on the quarterly financial reports, as well as a preliminary status report for the celebrity personal protection division for this quarter's board meeting."

A tight smile crawled across his face. "I'll be looking forward to reading it, too."

"I'm sure you will," she said, shaking her head.

"Well, with all that paperwork, I won't have to worry about you in the field." Meeks smirked as he checked the time on his watch.

"Don't start, and I will be checking in on Tiffany. I need to keep her apprised of things and make sure she understands we won't have anything on all that evidence we collected last night for a few days."

"That's a phone call. She has her new best friend as her personal bodyguard to hold her hand, remember?" he reminded.

"And she's my client, remember that? That status hasn't changed," she countered with her hands on her hips.

Meeks sighed. "As for our new status, until we figure out what this thing is between us…how serious it really is, maybe we should keep it to ourselves. You okay with that?"

"I'm okay with that," Francine said, nodding. She was

still unable to believe everything that had happened in the past twenty-four hours.

"I got to go," he said as he pulled her to her feet. "The guys are waiting, and I don't want to be late. Walk me to the door."

Francine complied and kissed him as he leaned his back against the door and kept her in his arms.

"If we don't stop this, I'll never get out of here," he said, pulling open the door only to find Farrah standing with her hand frozen in midair, ready to knock.

"So much for not telling anyone," Meeks said, looking over his shoulder at Francine who was shaking her head. "Good morning, Farrah."

"Good morning, you two." Farrah sauntered past Meeks and her sister and into the apartment, a slow, knowing smile spreading across her face. Her hair was pulled back into a tight bun, and she was holding a box of doughnuts and a file folder, which meant she'd planned to stay a while.

"I'm so not ready for this," Francine murmured.

"See you later," Meeks said before leaning down to give Francine a kiss that had her toes curling and body craving more.

Francine stood in the hallway and watched as Meeks disappeared into the elevator. She took a deep breath before moving into her apartment to deal with her sister.

Chapter 14

After pouring herself a cup of coffee, Farrah made her way into the living room and perched on the stool at the bar, giving her sister a quick once-over. Farrah was wearing a light blue Calvin Klein suit with blue stilettos, which meant that at some point during the day she would be seeing a judge. Farrah thought of blue as a power color that should be worn whenever she was in court or in front of a judge, regardless of the circumstances.

"*So*... I see you two have worked out your issues... finally. How was last night?" Farrah asked.

"Fine...nothing happened," Francine said, swiping her sister's cup and taking a sip.

"What! What do you mean nothing happened? Come on, sis. Spill," she urged as she went back into the kitchen to replace her stolen cup with another.

Francine pushed out a slow breath and dropped her shoulders, surrendering. She took the stool next to her sister, smiled and said, "Things started to heat up between us until we had to join you back at the theater, and it was so late when we left the office last night, we went to our separate apartments. He just dropped by this morning so we could talk. That's it. End of story."

Farrah sighed, opened the box she'd brought, extracted a chocolate cake doughnut and took a bite. "I'm so sorry, Cine," she said, chewing around the treat.

"No biggie…"

"We both know that's not true. So…how hot did it get?" Farrah asked, making her eyebrows dance.

Francine laughed, shaking her head and index finger.

"Seriously, Cine, what's going on with you two?"

"I don't know, but we're both finally ready to find out in spite of our business differences." Francine covered her face with both hands and released a low, excited scream like a kid receiving a gift he had been wanting.

Farrah laughed. "Good, you both deserve to be happy."

"Thanks, Farrah," she said as she reached and pulled her sister into a hug.

Farrah released Francine and leaned back into her chair. "So, is it safe to assume that you'll be addressing his 'Me Tarzan, You Jane' attitude?" she asked, laughing.

Francine giggled with her sister before finally saying, "We're having dinner Friday night, and that will definitely be a topic up for discussion—especially since he *told* me to go hold Tiffany's hand while he found out what was going on last night when we got back to the theater."

"Oh, no, he didn't?" Farrah said, placing her hand on her hip.

"Yes, he did."

"Tarzan!" Farrah threw her head back and laughed so hard she nearly fell off the stool. "He just can't seem to help himself."

"I know. Ever since I got shot, he and Dad have been

hovering. Then they wonder why I feel the need to prove to everyone that I'm fine." Francine released an exasperated sigh.

"You *are* fine, aren't you?" Farrah said, offering her sister a supportive smile.

"Yes, I am. I'll admit at first it was difficult adjusting… getting back to normal, but I have, and I really wish Meeks would recognize that already."

"Oh, sweetie." Farrah took her sister's hand and squeezed it. "It just doesn't matter. He's been watching over and pining after you for years. Meeks doesn't care that you're a double black belt and can shoot damn near any weapon known to man. He lets his fear get the best of him at times, but I'm sure you'll work it out. Even if you can't admit it yet, you two love each other too much for it not to."

Francine's emotions prevented her from speaking. She smiled and nodded as she wiped away tears she couldn't hold back. After a couple of moments, she pushed out a deep breath. "Enough about me and Meeks," Francine said as she reached for a glazed doughnut. "Why are you going to court?"

Farrah's forehead creased. "I'm not going to court today. What makes you ask that?"

"Really? Let's see. Blue power suit, sky high heels and your hair pulled back so tight my head hurts," she said as she washed down her doughnut with coffee.

"Yeah, well, Miss Smarty Pants, I'm not in court today. I have a meeting with Judge Cutter," she said with a smug expression.

Francine frowned and shuddered slightly at the memory of the man who, after meeting her for the first time, eyed her up and down at a party and actually licked his lips and winked at her. He'd followed all that up with a sloppy pass. "Roger Cutter…why are you meeting with him?"

"He was the presiding judge on a couple of cases brought against Tiffany's former security agency, and I'm hoping there's something he can share without crossing any lines."

"Roger Cutter not crossing ethical lines? That would be a first," Francine said, not even trying to hide her dislike for the man.

Judge Cutter was new to the bench. While he was ten years older than the sisters, his movie-star good looks and shoulder-length blond hair made him look like he was much younger. He'd been appointed after his predecessor died unexpectedly last year from a mysterious virus. He had also been one of Farrah's law professors, and he'd flirted with her throughout her senior year. While Farrah didn't think the attention he paid her was that big of a deal since he'd never crossed any lines, it amounted to sexual harassment in Francine's eyes.

"I'm hoping he'll be able to shed some light on a few things that have come to my attention."

Francine perked up. "Like what…what did you find out? Anything about Tiffany's boyfriends?" Francine reached for the hair clip that Meeks had removed the night before and put her hair back up. A smile she couldn't have stopped if she wanted to spread across her face as she remembered what happened after he removed the clip. *Focus, girl.*

While they had a crack research team at their disposal, and Robert and Meeks were very good at what they did, no one could dig up dirt like Farrah, and no one had her contacts. She always went beyond the surface of any investigation, especially one that piqued her interest like this one had.

Farrah pushed a loose strand of hair behind her ear and picked up the manila folder she'd brought with her. "Well, it seems that the lovely Tiffany failed to mention that bodyguard boyfriend number one, a Mr. Lee Jergens, whom she dated off and on for two years, was freelance, but had been her exclusive bodyguard for six months before they started dating. When Tiffany's first movie blew up, they moved her security to the Bluebonnet Agency, which Mr. Morgan owns a pretty big portion of, too—something he failed to mention," she said, shaking her head and rolling her eyes.

"Seriously?" Francine coughed and nearly choked on her coffee. "How did the guys miss this?"

"It was a connection he tried his damnedest to keep covered up," she explained, flipping through her files. "Believe me, it was buried deep under several shell corporations. I'm sure they would have found it eventually, but I reached out to a couple of forensic accountants I know in the banking industry that owed me a few favors and had them take a closer look into Tiffany's and Mr. Morgan's financials. They found several discrepancies with Mr. Morgan, so I had them track the money, and it gets worse. He's been pilfering Tiffany's accounts for years, too."

Francine got up and walked into her kitchen. She pulled out eggs, cheese and a prepackaged veggie bowl from her refrigerator.

"Wow. Wait, if Bill Morgan owns a portion of Bluebonnet, why did he want to change security companies and give us the business? I mean, losing that contract means he lost millions," Francine said as she reached for a couple of plates and grabbed a small pan out of the cabinet. She started tapping eggs against the countertop. "I'm going to make an omelet. Want one?"

"No, thanks," Farrah said, waving off her sister. "That's just it, he didn't—Tiffany did. She may be young, but she's still the boss. Besides, I'm willing to bet she didn't even know about Mr. Morgan's stake in Bluebonnet. She probably just wanted to get away from all her ex-boyfriends."

"So was Tiffany still dating Jergens once they moved to Bluebonnet?" Francine asked as she cracked open two eggs into her heated pan, broke the yokes and added the cheese and veggie mixture.

"Well, Jergens got a job with Bluebonnet to try to stay close to her. However, Bluebonnet had something else in mind," Farrah said.

"Let me guess the rest," Francine said as she flipped her omelet closed. "Jergens wasn't put on Tiffany's security detail, and she moved on but he didn't." Francine slid her omelet onto a plate. She let her food cool while she put her ingredients away and dirty dishes in the dishwasher.

"Basically, that's what happened. He tried to get both Bill and Tiffany to hire him back as her personal security freelancer so he could stay close to Tiffany, but Tiffany had already moved into an intimate relationship with bodyguard Sam Mitch, and she didn't want Jergens around complicating things."

Francine shook her head. "I should say not. Do we know where Mr. Jergens is now?" she asked, retaking the seat next to her sister and biting into her eggs.

"Not yet. I put a team on it first thing this morning," Farrah said, reaching over, picking up the fork and taking a bite of her sister's omelet.

"You know I hate it when you do that," Francine said.

Farrah laughed. "I know."

"Did I not ask you if you wanted me to make you one?" Francine snatched back her fork.

"Dang, Cine, I just wanted a bite," Farrah complained.

"A *big* bite!" Francine said.

"All right… I'm sorry. It's really good," Farrah said, giving her a cheeky smile.

Francine returned her smile and said, "Thanks. So, has

Robert been brought up to speed on any of this?" Francine asked.

"Yeah, I talked to him about it this morning," she said.

Francine's eyes narrowed at her sister. "Farrah...did you spend the night with Robert?" she asked.

Francine knew that Robert and Farrah had a pretty obvious and intense flirtation going on, but that's all she thought it was. After all, her sister had been pretty vocal about not dating playboys, and everyone knew Robert was one of the biggest on the planet. The man was rich and gorgeous, tall, had a perfect athletic body, fair skin that was always tanned and crystal blue eyes. He could and did have just about any woman that he wanted. And it was pretty clear that he wanted Farrah.

"Calm down, Cine," Farrah said with a chuckle. "And no, I didn't. We were both in the gym working out this morning, so I told him then. He plans to tell Meeks everything after they meet with the team, before they leave for Beaumont to handle the chemical plant's annual security reviews."

"That should make our dinner Friday night even more interesting," Francine said.

"Yep, and you know he's going to try to get you to walk away from this case again. And this time...he'll use his *secret weapon* on you," Farrah said, wiggling her eyebrows. "A weapon that won't be a secret long, and one I don't think you'll be immune to."

Francine tried to ignore her sister, but she knew she was right. Now that she and Meeks had acknowledged that there was something pretty significant between them in spite of their business differences, Francine was afraid he would try to use it to his advantage. "You know, the best defense is a good offense," she said with a wicked smile.

Farrah returned her smile and winked. "That's my girl."

Chapter 15

Meeks had been having a difficult time concentrating on work since he'd left Francine's place that morning. All he could think about was how beautiful she was. How she tasted, what it felt like to have her lips wrapped around his throbbing manhood. His wayward thoughts had him fidgeting in his chair. Thank goodness Robert was wrapping up the meeting for him; otherwise, he'd have to do it from a seated position.

Robert had just dismissed the team when he pulled Meeks aside and brought him up to speed on Tiffany's case.

"Damn it. I knew we should have walked away from this one. It's bad enough that this girl is being stalked. Now we find out that her manager—former guardian—has been stealing money from her, too. This is going to be messy," Meeks said as he walked into his office and made his way around to his desk. He sat in the large leather chair behind his father's antique cherry wood desk. Meeks had kept his father's old office basically the same since the day he'd moved into it.

"Why the hell didn't you pick up on any of this during your initial search? Are you losing your touch?"

Robert's forehead creased. "I'm going to pretend you didn't just ask me that. We both know how deep Farrah's connections go in the financial and legal worlds, not to mention they're mostly women that she works with. And you know how good females are at getting the dirt on people."

Both men laughed.

"True. Sorry." Meeks sighed. "Man, I'm getting a bad feeling about this case, and I want Francine as far away from this as possible."

"Well, you know that's not going to happen," Robert said before he took a drink from his water bottle.

Meeks got up from his desk and gazed out his window. "We'll see. Ever since Francine got shot, she seems more determined than ever to prove something."

"Prove what?" Robert asked.

"I wish I knew," Meeks said, turning back to face his friend.

"I know you two are having some issues right now…"

A wide smile crept across Meeks's face. He couldn't help but remember how he and Francine had started their night. Meeks let his mind wander to how it felt to kiss those beautiful full lips, to run his tongue up her inner thigh and how she screamed his name—

"Meeks…"

Meeks snapped out of his trance before his thoughts continued down a path that would have had his body responding in a way that would embarrass both men.

"What?" Meeks asked, returning to his chair where he started checking his email.

Distraction…distraction is the key.

Robert stared at Meeks for a moment and tilted his head to one side. "You didn't….did you?" After a few moments his mouth dropped. "You did!"

"So who did you assign to find this Jergens?" Meeks asked.

"Jasper. And nice try on changing the subject," Robert said as he got up and headed for the door. "I hope you know what you're doing. Francine is not one to be played with, my friend."

"Don't I know it," Meeks murmured, flicking his pen against the desk.

Meeks spent a few moments trying to figure out how to convince Francine to bow out of this case. It might have been months since she'd been shot, but to Meeks, the pain and fear of that day were still very fresh. Just the thought of her getting hurt again stopped him in his tracks. While he knew it wouldn't be easy, he figured now that they were finally willing to explore their feelings for each other, he had a lot more say in what she did. Meeks hadn't told Francine how he felt about her yet, but he certainly intended to. Surprisingly, he was actually looking forward to it.

Francine walked into her apartment, wiping sweat from her brow. She had been determined not to let last night's craziness interfere with her daily exercise routine. She went to her kitchen, removing the clip from her head and releasing her hair before retrieving a bottle of water from her refrigerator and putting it to her lips. Francine was halfway through her drink when she heard her iPad ringing; she was receiving a FaceTime call. She sat at the bar, pulled it open and waited for the connection. Francine smiled the moment she saw a ponytailed version of herself—only this one had hazel eyes.

"Well, it's about time you returned one of my many

phone calls," Francine said, while somehow both smiling and frowning.

"Good morning to you, too, sis," Felicia said.

"It's afternoon here, which reminds me—where the hell are you, Felicia?"

Felicia stared at her sister and shook her head slowly.

Francine sighed and smiled. "Sorry, sis."

Felicia gifted her sister with a wide smile. "I love and miss you, too," she said before taking a sip from a World's Greatest Sisters coffee mug. "I'm in Jeju, South Korea, and before you start, yes, Mom and Dad know, and I've only been here a couple of days. We had to hit the ground running so we could beat the rain and no, I still can't tell you why I'm here or what I'm working on. I work for the CIA, remember?"

Francine threw her head back and laughed. "You know this triplet psychic thing we got going on just gets worse the older we get."

"Tell me about it," she agreed, taking another sip from her cup.

"I see you still have your mug," Francine said. The memory of when they "made" them flashed through her mind.

"Of course. I'll never forget Farrah coming home all pissed off because the store only had mugs that read World's Greatest Sister, so she insisted that we use permanent markers to add the *s*." Felicia danced her cup in front of the camera. "Don't you?"

"Yes, I do," Francine said, smiling.

The security phone next to her door rang.

Francine frowned as she checked her watch; she wasn't due to see Meeks until Friday. She wasn't expecting anyone, and she rarely got any surprise outside visitors.

"I hear you're being buzzed. You expecting company?"

Felicia asked, giving her sister a silly grin much like Farrah's when she was having naughty thoughts.

"No…not yet, anyway. I see you and Farrah have been talking. How soon after she left my place this morning did she call you?"

"She barely made it to her apartment," she said, laughing.

The security phone rang again.

"Go get that. Don't keep him waiting," she said, making her eyebrows dance. "Besides, I've got to go anyway. I'll call again soon… I promise."

"Okay, be careful, Felicia. Love you," Francine said.

"Love you, too, and give Meeks my best," she said, giggling as she signed off.

Francine shook her head as she went to answer the phone. "What's up, Stan?" she asked the building's security guard.

"Sorry to disturb you, Ms. Blake, but there's a Jasmine Black here to see you," he informed her.

"What's she doing here?" Francine whispered, looking at the phone as if she expected an answer. She returned it to her ear and said, "Send her up, Stan."

Francine hung up the phone and ran to her bathroom where she quickly wiped her face, brushed her hair and pulled it back up into a high ponytail. She grabbed her body spray and squirted herself twice just as her doorbell rang.

"Well, at least I don't look too crazy," she said to her reflection. Francine made her way to the door to greet her guest.

She plastered a smile on her face and opened her door.

Jasmine Black stood in the doorway, looking beautiful in a gray, printed Vera Wang scoop dress and strappy stilettos in the same color. "Jasmine, nice to see you again. Please come in."

"Thank you, and please forgive the intrusion," she said.

"No problem. I was just finishing up my workout, so forgive my appearance." Francine gestured to the workout gear she was wearing. "Please, have a seat."

Jasmine's gaze swept the area in a matter of seconds. "You have a beautiful home. I can't get over how much the layout reminds me of Meeks's place."

"Thanks," Francine said. "Can I get you something to drink?"

"No thanks," Jasmine said, taking a seat on Francine's sofa. "I hate the way our introduction went yesterday, so I just thought we could start over. You know, clear the air, since we'll all be working together." Jasmine gave her a smile. "I can only imagine how truly angry you must have been, being blindsided like that by a client. I wouldn't like it either, and I certainly wouldn't have handled it as well as you did."

"Thanks."

"Also, I'd hate for my relationship with Meeks to cause problems between us."

Francine took a seat in the chair across from Jasmine. "I didn't realize you and Meeks had a relationship. I mean, I know you two have history, but that's what I thought it was…*history.* Are you telling me it's not?" Francine asked with raised eyebrows.

"Of course not," she practically purred. "Our relationship is friendly at best. We didn't end things on the best of terms, although—" she traced a finger across her cleavage "—I do plan to rectify that fact as soon as possible. You know, so our working together won't be so…*awkward.* Now, if you weren't in the picture, and you obviously are, I wouldn't be opposed to another brief affair," she said, laughing. "The man is quite—" she shivered as though experiencing a mild orgasm "—well, you don't need me to tell you what he is."

"No… I don't," Francine said, giving her a smile that spoke volumes.

Jasmine tilted her head and smirked. "Good. At least you're not denying you're together," she said, flipping her long hair off her shoulders.

"Of course I'm not," Francine said as she crossed her arms under her chest. "Like you said, your relationship with Meeks is friendly as it should be. There's no reason for us to play games."

Jasmine's smile didn't quite reach her green eyes. "True, you don't need to worry about me. I could never give Meeks what he wants. Not that it's any of my business, but I can't see how you could, either."

A stab of concern settled in Francine's gut.

"I mean, you're just as strong and independent as I am," Jasmine said. Then she added, "At least, from everything I've heard. And you really seem to love what you do. Staying at home barefoot and pregnant, waiting for your man to come home every day, just doesn't seem like it's your style. It damn sure isn't mine."

An edge of doubt about their ability to work out their business differences crept in. Francine had always had these concerns about Meeks's thoughts on gender roles; she thought they could be a little extreme. That was part of the same reason she had kept her distance for so long.

"No, you don't know me," Francine said. "People have many sides to them, and they can want a multitude of things. I'm sure it wouldn't surprise you one bit what some people are capable of under the right circumstances," she advised.

"Especially if one thinks *Meeks* is the right circumstance," Jasmine said, giving Francine a smile that said there was more to her statement than she wanted to share.

Francine checked her watch and looked back at Jasmine, who grinned.

"I won't hold you. I'm sure you have better things to do other than to sit here talking to me." Her gaze took in everything in the area once again, but lingered on the side table where a picture of Meeks with Francine and her sisters sat. "Besides, I have another stop I need to make before I have to go meet Tiffany. I'm canceling another date. He'll stop asking me soon."

"So you're dating someone?" Francine asked, tilting her head slightly.

The other woman laughed. "I wouldn't say we were dating…not really. But a girl's got needs, and it's really hard finding someone who can handle being with women like us." Jasmine shrugged her shoulders. "Anyway, the little darling has another party that she just *has* to make an appearance at."

"I'm sure she does," Francine said. "Don't cancel your date. I'll cover Tiffany's event."

"Seriously?" Jasmine frowned.

"Of course. Despite what some people think, Tiffany is my client."

Jasmine threw her head back and laughed. "Yeah, Meeks does have a strong protective gene when it comes to his women."

"Yes, he does."

Jasmine stood and said, "Thanks again for tonight, and I'm really glad we cleared the air."

"Me, too," Francine replied, following her guest to the door.

A small voice inside Francine's head told her she'd better be careful. It was pretty clear that Jasmine just might think she and Meeks had some unfinished business.

Chapter 16

The elevator door opened to the top floor of Francine's building, and she paused and her breath caught when she laid eyes on Meeks. He was giving her an intense glare. "I'd kiss you senseless if I didn't want to strangle you right now."

Francine raised her chin, put her hands on her hips and said, "Missed you, too."

"You just can't help yourself, can you? And it should be illegal to wear that dress after two in the morning, let alone after six."

"Excuse me?"

"You heard me," he replied. He was shirtless, leaning against his apartment doorframe and looking like some fair-skinned Greek god at six in the morning—a time when most humans barely looked alive. But there he stood, shaking his head and giving Francine that disapproving look he knew she hated. "What happened to doing paperwork?"

"What are you doing back so early? I didn't expect to

see you until later," she said, fishing her key out of her handbag as she continued on to her apartment.

"I bet." He swiped the key from her and unlocked and opened her door.

"It's been a long night," she said, placing her purse on the antique side table that sat in her foyer. "And I don't have the time or the energy for this."

She had finally been able to get Tiffany to leave the third after-hours club, where Francine had to toss a couple of overzealous fans out of their VIP section and call it a night. It had taken her another hour to brief her replacement, do one final perimeter check of Tiffany's house and drag her tired butt across town to her apartment. The last thing she needed was to deal with Meeks's judgmental behind.

"As for my outfit, you and I both know it's perfectly appropriate for my assignment," she declared as she watched him enter and close the door behind him.

"An assignment you hijacked," he accused while leaning against her door.

"I did no such thing," she protested, standing a few feet away from him. "Jasmine had a date and she didn't want to cancel, so the paperwork had to wait. I'm nearly done anyway. Someone had to cover."

All Francine wanted to do was take off the low-cut black sequined minidress that she'd never dare wear, then take the fastest shower known to man before climbing into bed for some long overdue sleep. The last thing she needed was to hear the same old crap from Meeks, although she really was happy to see him.

"A date?"

"Yes, you have a problem with that?" she challenged, standing with her hand on her hip.

"I could care less about Jasmine's dating life. *She* had

a job to do, but if she couldn't she should have contacted Davis so *he* could have found a replacement. It didn't have to be you, Cine," he protested.

"It most certainly did," she shot back as she slowly moved farther into her living room. "Tiffany's my client, and it's my job!"

Meeks straightened to his full six-two height, which gave him a half-foot advantage over Francine, whose five-inch heels were now dangling from her fingers. He walked toward her, holding the towel that was draped around his neck. His skin glistened, and sweat dripped from his head and landed on his muscular chest. He had obviously just finished a workout, something he often did when he was angry or annoyed. The moment Meeks's piercing dark eyes swept over her body, Francine's nipples hardened and all her blood seemed to rush south—an all-too-familiar response that seemed to intensify whenever they were arguing.

"It wasn't your job," he challenged, glaring down at her with his hands in his pockets. "You have been assigned backup for at least two more months for a reason. Hell, if it were up to me, you'd stay in the office."

"Well, it's not up to you. And again, Tiffany is *my* client. Anyway, as CEO, I'm supposed to maintain relationships with our clients, even if that means doing so in the field," Francine proclaimed as she sat down on her cream-colored leather sofa, dropping her shoes next to it. She was happy that she'd thought to remove her jewelry and gun and place them in her purse before leaving the party. She yanked off her wig and began extracting the numerous pins necessary to keep her long, thick mane in place underneath it.

With each pin she removed, the pain in her head eased a little. Francine's dark, naturally curly hair fell past her shoulders to rest in the center of her lower back. She smirked as she watched Meeks's eyes fill with desire as he watched her ruffle her hair. Even when they were kids, he'd loved it when she wore it down. Francine took a deep breath, closed her eyes and lay on her left side.

If only the pain in Francine's side could be eased as easily as the one in her head; she felt like she was being scraped by a large shard of glass. Francine refused to address that pain in front of Meeks, so taking a pill was out of the question. Instead, she began lightly rubbing her side and hip, hoping he wouldn't notice.

"Shit! I knew it."

He noticed.

"Don't start," she said without opening her eyes. She pulled down the throw from the back of the sofa to cover herself from shoulders to feet. Francine could feel Meeks staring at her, but she kept her eyes shut.

Meeks could feel his anger coming to the forefront. "So much for following your doctor's advice," Meeks mumbled as he watched her grimace while trying to shift her body on the sofa. He made his way into Francine's bathroom to collect her pain medicine. Then he went into her kitchen and retrieved a cold pack and a bottle of water from the refrigerator and a glass from her cabinet. Meeks knelt down beside Francine, and several moments of silence ticked by. Just as she was falling deeper into sleep, he pressed the cold pack to her side.

Meeks watched as Francine forced her beautiful green eyes open. He made sure his glare spoke to his displeasure. He was angry because she had gone out in the field and overdone it again. What had him angriest was that something could have happened to her and he would have been out of town...again; only this time, it would have taken longer to get to her. Francine still didn't get it. She was his whole world.

"Here," he said as he handed her two of her pills and the glass of water that he'd poured for her. "Take them."

She sat up slightly, took the pills and tossed them down with a few sips of water. "Thanks," she said before closing her eyes, breaking their connection.

"Should I expect you for the three o'clock staff meeting this afternoon?" he asked as he leaned in closer.

"Umm...yeah," she murmured.

"I may be annoyed with you right now, but I'm happy you're okay. Get some rest, baby," he said in a softer tone before giving her a gentle kiss on the lips.

Francine's eyes opened slowly. "We still on for dinner tonight?" she asked in a voice barely above a whisper.

He held her gaze and cupped the side of her face with his right hand. "I sure hope so, but only if you're feeling better." Francine sighed and the corner of her mouth curved upward as she closed her eyes.

Meeks adjusted the plush throw covering her body, tucking her in as she slipped into a most welcome slumber. Meeks continued to stand over her for a moment longer. He tilted his head and watched as her perfect full lips made a small pout as she slept. His eyes followed her jawline down her neck. Meeks always thought she had the most beautiful neck he'd ever seen. Not to mention the rest of her perfect body—full breasts that were soft to his touch, a round, firm butt and long legs that just seemed to go on forever. At that very moment, he would have done anything to have those legs wrapped around his waist. His sex was as hard as concrete.

Meeks took a quick detour to the kitchen and set up her coffee machine. Francine's apartment was one of four on the top floor—one at each corner of the building. All the apartments had identical floor plans: a wide entry that housed a half bath and a coat closet and led to a huge open-concept room with a gourmet kitchen. The floor-to-ceiling collapsible windows allowed for open access onto a balcony that was made for entertaining. Each apartment also contained four bedrooms, each with en suite bathrooms, and a separate office space, which could tempt even the most dedicated executive to never leave home again.

Meeks looked at Francine's sleeping form one final time before leaving her apartment and locking up. He headed back to his own place for a very cold shower.

Before he could make it to his bathroom, his phone rang. He checked the screen and smirked before he answered, "What's up?"

"Everything cool?" Jeremy, his assistant, asked. "I see she's in."

"Yeah, we're cool," Meeks replied, stripping down to the bare minimum. "Thanks for the heads-up."

"Not like you gave me much choice," Jeremy said, chuckling. "Didn't you tell me you wanted her tracked from now on?"

"Absolutely. As long as she keeps playing full-time agent, I want to know if she's putting herself in any danger."

"You headed down?"

"In a bit. I need to hit the shower first," Meeks said before ending the call and placing his phone on the edge of the sink.

When he stepped under the spray, the cold water pelted his body, putting a cool damper on the heat that had flared the moment he had laid eyes on Francine.

The sheer blinds that Meeks had closed prevented the afternoon sun from piercing the wall of windows of the glass high-rise building where they both worked and lived. Francine tossed and turned in what felt like a confined space. Finally, she reached for her phone to dismiss her screaming alarm at the same time the aroma of freshly brewed coffee assaulted her senses.

She stretched, checking for any lingering pains and released a deep sigh after finding none. "Looks like I owe you another one, Meeks," Francine said to herself as she pulled off the throw, smiled up at the Vincent van Gogh painting she'd recently purchased at Sotheby's that was now hanging on her wall and headed to her kitchen to pour a huge cup of Juan Valdez's best.

As she sipped the contents, Francine dialed Meeks. At the sound of his voice, she smiled. "Thank you."

"Are you feeling better?" Meeks asked, his tone just as soft as their last kiss.

"Much," she said, trying to temper the excitement she felt at the sound of his voice.

"See you in a few."

Francine finished her coffee, showered and dressed in the agency uniform. Meeks might still be a little upset with her for covering for Jasmine last night and she was sure he would have more to say about it. But Francine had the perfect change of subject—the outfit she'd wear to dinner, which she hoped would ensure their evening would end on a much sweeter note.

Francine exited the elevator onto the floor where their office was housed and ran into a nervous-looking Kelly. "Good, I was coming to find you."

"Find me, why? What's up?"

"Miss Tiffany's stalker struck again."

"What…when?"

"Last night." Kelly was leading her toward the conference room. "While…" She stopped talking the moment they entered the conference room.

Meeks was standing next to the windows with his legs slightly apart, his arms folded at his chest with a deep frown on his face. Jasmine was sitting at the conference room table, surprisingly wearing their same uniform with her arms folded and lips stuck out like a child being scolded. Robert sat to her right, looking like he'd rather be anywhere but there. Farrah, who was looking beautiful in a formfitting lavender dress, a fact that clearly didn't go unnoticed by Robert, came and stood next to her.

"What's going on?" Francine asked, her eyes scanning the room.

"If that'll be all?" Kelly asked.

Meeks gave a curt nod and she scampered out, closing the door behind her. "That's what's going on," he said, pointing to a note sealed in one of their evidence bags. It had been created by pasting magazine clippings together. Francine walked over to the table and read the document. "'Sorry I missed you at Red's—'" the last club they'd visited "'—Oh, well, next time. I thought telling people you were there would have been more of a distraction. I underestimated your bodyguard. That won't happen again.'"

"Where did this come from?" she asked, staring down at the note.

"Tiffany's maid found it this morning in the coat she wore last night," Jasmine explained, her eyes darting between her and Meeks. "Bill Morgan called me this morning as soon as they found it."

"He called you first?" Francine asked, turning her attention to Jasmine.

"Who the hell cares why he called her first?" Meeks bellowed at Francine. "You're missing the damn point. You aggravated your injury at that club last night where Tiffany's stalker was, a place *you* shouldn't have been. You didn't have enough significant backup."

"Ha...significant backup, as in *you*?" she asked sarcastically.

"Damn right!"

"This is my case," Francine threw back, pointing at herself. "I'm fine and I did have the *appropriate* backup and you know it. Stop making this about me!" Francine hated that her wayward body was so aware of Meeks in that moment.

They both stood glaring at each other, each with one hand resting on the hip that held their gun. The energy flowing between them was almost visible. It was like their anger and passion were at war.

"You don't see that every day," Jasmine murmured.

"Yes, we do," Farrah and Robert declared in unison.

Farrah gave Robert a tight smile. "Look, Cine, the note just came in, so let's go take it down to the forensic team," she said, grabbing her sister's hand. "Jasmine, why don't you go remind Bill of the proper notification protocols, and Robert, I'll leave you to deal with Meeks?"

"Thanks," Robert replied to their quickly retreating forms.

Chapter 17

Meeks opened the door to Francine, who was about to knock. She wore a low-cut black mini wrap dress with a pair of red heels that made her legs look exceptionally long, and her beautiful hair was hanging down her back just the way he liked it. His heart began to race from a combination of gratitude, desire and fear. Gratitude that she'd agreed to keep their date that night after that afternoon's display of madness, desire for the woman who stood before him and fear that Jasmine's presence could taint the beautiful evening he'd planned.

"Perfect," Meeks murmured.

Jasmine laughed and walked past Francine. "Have a nice evening, you two," she said as she made her way over to the elevator.

Francine entered Meeks's apartment without looking back at Jasmine. Meeks closed the door, doing his best to block the dramatic exit Jasmine was clearly trying to provide.

Francine stopped and turned to face him. Meeks searched her face for any indication of what she might be thinking, but as usual Francine covered her feelings with a smile that didn't quite reach her eyes.

"Unexpected houseguest?" she asked him, gesturing to the lipstick-stained glass sitting on the bar.

Meeks walked into the kitchen. "To say the least," he said, picking up the glass and placing it in the dishwasher. He returned and stood with his hands in his pockets in front of Francine and smiled down at her. "I'm really glad we didn't let what happened earlier today ruin our plans, although I feel a little underdressed," he said, looking down at the black jeans and T-shirt he was wearing, "because you look absolutely beautiful."

Francine eyed him up and down, biting the corner of her lip before offering him a slow, sexy smile. "Thank you. And I've always liked you in jeans and a T-shirt," she replied, as he watched her breasts rising and falling slowly.

Unable to hold back any longer, Meeks removed his right hand from his pocket and slid the back of it down her cheek. He knew that the fire raging inside him would consume them both much sooner than he'd like if he didn't have at least a small taste of her. Meeks held her gaze, searching for any signs of doubt as he lowered his head to hers. Francine remained perfectly still, parting her lips slightly, and Meeks captured them in a passionate kiss that only intensified his needs; with his hands buried in her hair, he devoured her mouth as though this would be his only opportunity.

Francine's hands slid up his chest and around his neck as she pressed her body against his. Meeks knew that if he didn't pull back soon, the evening he'd planned would take a delightful detour that needed to be put off just a bit longer. He reached behind his neck and unclasped her hands and slowly stepped out of her hold.

"If we keep this up, we'll never get to dinner," he said, holding her hands.

Francine looked over into the kitchen and laughed. "Well, it does look like you went through an awful lot of trouble. Smells like your mother's sauce."

Meeks gave her another quick kiss before he started moving around the kitchen, preparing to serve dinner.

"You sure I can't do anything to help?" Francine asked.

"Nope," Meeks said as he removed two bowls filled with a green salad mix from the refrigerator. After adding his homemade dressing, Meeks handed Francine a bowl and said, "Bon appétit."

"Mmmm, this is so good." Francine closed her eyes for a moment as she took a bite. "I love your dressing. You have to give me the recipe."

Meeks reached over and gave her a not-so-quick kiss on the corner of her mouth, using his tongue to swipe away some of the dressing that rested there. "Delicious," he said, giving her a wicked smile. "And I'll consider sharing my recipe with you if you're a good girl…a very good girl."

Francine covered her mouth to hold in a laugh.

Meeks poured the sauce over the plated noodles and placed the plates on the bar. He took the seat next to Francine and took a sip of his wine. "I hope you like it."

Francine swirled the noodles around her fork and took a bite. She swallowed and smiled. "Meeks, this is wonderful. Your mom taught you well," she said as she took another bite.

"Thanks. Other than grilling steaks and preparing a few breakfast dishes, this is by far my favorite thing to make." Meeks reached for the bottle and topped off her glass. "You

Send For
2 FREE BOOKS
Today!

I accept your offer!

Please send me two
free novels and two mystery
gifts (gifts worth about $10).
I understand that these books
are completely free—even
the shipping and handling will
be paid—and I am under no
obligation to purchase anything,
ever, as explained on the back
of this card.

168/368 HDL GHT3

Please Print

FIRST NAME

LAST NAME

ADDRESS

APT.#   CITY

STATE/PROV.   ZIP/POSTAL CODE

Visit us online at
www.ReaderService.com

◄ Detach card and mail today. No stamp needed. ◄   © 2015 HARLEQUIN ENTERPRISES LIMITED. ® and ™ are trademarks owned and used by the trademark owner and/or its licensee. Printed in the U.S.A.

K-815-GF15

Send For
2 FREE BOOKS
Today!

I accept your offer!

Please send me two
free novels and two mystery
gifts (gifts worth about $10).
I understand that these books
are completely free—even
the shipping and handling will
be paid—and I am under no
obligation to purchase anything,
ever, as explained on the back
of this card.

168/368 HDL GHT3

Please Print

FIRST NAME

LAST NAME

ADDRESS

APT.#   CITY

STATE/PROV.   ZIP/POSTAL CODE

Visit us online at
www.ReaderService.com

know how much our mom wanted to make sure we could take care of ourselves until we found wives."

Meeks's nonchalant comment reminded Francine of the conversation she'd just had with Jasmine, and her appetite began to wane.

Francine pushed her plate forward and wiped her mouth with her napkin.

Meeks frowned. "You done already?" he asked between bites. "You still have half a plate, and we both know you can eat more than that."

Francine gave him a half smile and said, "It really was wonderful, but I'm stuffed." She got up, taking her plate with her, and started cleaning up the kitchen.

"You don't have to do that," Meeks said as he placed another bite of food in his mouth.

"You know the Blake rule. You don't cook, but if you eat, you clean," she said, laughing.

Meeks finished his meal and helped Francine tidy the kitchen in spite of her protests. She decided not to let his comment about finding a wife ruin the rest of their evening, so they shared another bottle of wine while they relaxed on his sofa.

"So… Jasmine…" Francine asked.

"What about Jasmine?" Meeks replied as he took another sip of his wine and sat farther back into his seat.

Francine sat forward and placed her glass on the table. She turned toward Meeks. "Is this how you want to handle this…really?" Francine asked, crossing her arms and giving him a defiant stare.

"Damn, you're beautiful when you're mad," Meeks said, eyeing her up and down and giving her that sexy smile she loved.

"Stop looking at me like that when I'm trying to get some answers," she snapped.

Meeks laughed.

Francine ignored what her body was telling her and continued to glare at him.

He sighed, sat forward and placed his glass on the table next to hers. "All right, what do you want to know?"

"What was she doing here?"

Meeks unfolded her arms and intertwined their fingers. "It was nothing. She just wanted to clear the air between us since we'll be working together," he explained as he circled her palm with his thumb before lightly kissing the back of her hands.

Francine's body immediately responded to his touch. Her nipples hardened, and her breasts felt heavy. Francine crossed her legs, trying to ease the pressure—she could tell by Meeks's smile that the move didn't go unnoticed.

"Really? You think that's all she wants?" she asked with raised eyebrows.

"Why, did she mention something different to you when you two met earlier?" he asked, raising an eyebrow.

"No, she didn't."

"Were you going to tell me she came to see you?" he asked, his eyes not leaving her face.

"Were you?" she challenged.

"Of course. There's nothing between me and Jasmine, Francine."

Francine gave him a knowing look, and he amended his statement. "Not anymore," he clarified.

Francine nodded, but she wasn't so sure if she believed him one hundred percent, although she desperately wanted to.

"Besides, it was never anything serious. We dated off and on—mostly off—for about a year, but things didn't work out. We both just wanted different things out of life."

I could never give Meeks what he wanted. Jasmine's words popped into Francine's head.

"I've been thinking about you all damn day," Meeks said, kissing Francine's hands again. "Can we talk about Jasmine and anything else that you think we should another time?"

Meeks's words and touch broke through Francine's thoughts. "I've been thinking about and missing you, too," she replied.

He swept her off her feet. "I think it's time for us to pick up where we left off the other night, don't you?"

Francine answered him with her kiss as he carried her into his bedroom. She kicked off her heels as soon as they entered the room, which screamed testosterone: oatmeal-colored walls, dark wood furnishings that complemented the hardwood floors perfectly, and an oversize bed dressed in chocolate-and-cream sheets. The one noteworthy item that caught her attention was a picture of a naked, dark-skinned couple sitting with their bodies intertwined and held together by a chain. By the way the female subject's face was contorted, it was clear that she was in the throes of passion. The picture had been framed in a hand-carved wooden box and hung above his bed. Francine recognized the frame immediately—it was the first piece she had ever sold.

Meeks stopped in front of his bed when he realized what had captured Francine's attention. "I bought that a few years ago."

"How?" she asked, her eyes wide with wonder. "I sold that frame to an artist in Europe. At the time he had no idea how he'd even use the frame."

"Your mom told my mom about it, and my mom mentioned it to me. *I* wanted to own your first piece. So I contacted the artist and commissioned that picture with the stipulation that it be placed in your frame."

Francine always knew that he'd supported her art, but she had had no idea to what degree.

Meeks placed her on her feet but didn't release her as he said, "I think your woodworks are spectacular."

Francine closed her eyes, dropped her head and shook it slowly. "You're unbelievable. Thank you," she said without raising her head to meet his gaze.

Meeks took the index finger of his right hand, placed it under her chin and raised her head.

Francine opened her eyes, which were glossy with unshed tears, and looked into his. "You are the one who is unbelievable," he whispered before lowering his head to capture her lips again.

Francine rose up on her tiptoes to meet his kiss. Moments later she pulled away and took a step back. Meeks watched as Francine slowly untied the bow at the side of her dress. As the dress fell open, a hot-pink lace strapless bra and matching lace panties made an appearance and captured his attention. Francine used the tips of her fingers to act as a guide for his desire-filled eyes to follow as he explored her body while she stood before him. Meeks made Francine feel bold, yet…safe.

"You're b-beautiful," Meeks stammered as he continued to stare.

Francine let her dress fall to the floor and stood still as Meeks took his fill of the lush curves of her body. She bit her lower lip, feeling excited and brave about her next move. She unhooked her bra and let it fall to the floor and repeated her previous exploration, touching her neck, collarbone and breast before placing her hands on her hips and widening her stance.

"Damn," Meeks whispered.

As his gaze roamed her body, his breathing grew audibly labored as the crotch of his pants expanded, and her nipples hardened. Francine felt overwhelmed by her need and an emotion she wasn't ready to put a name to yet. She only hoped that her wetness didn't make its way down her legs.

"Those panties, are they your favorite pair?" Meeks asked in a husky tone.

"No," Francine said, her voice barely above a whisper.

"Good!" Meeks dropped to his knees in front of Francine, stared up into her eyes and ripped them in half. He placed Francine's left leg over his shoulder, grabbed her buttocks with both hands and took her hard and fast with his mouth. Meeks licked, bit, teased and sucked Francine's flesh until she shook and screamed his name with her release. He scooped up her limp body and placed her in the center of the bed.

He stood and retrieved a condom from his nightstand before he took off the remainder of his clothes, tossing them to the side, then sheathing himself within that thin wall of protection. When he lowered his head and used his nose to push aside the beautiful hair that was covering her nipple before he took one breast into his mouth, pulling and sucking in a manner that had Francine arching her back to offer him more of herself, he nearly lost what was left of his control. He repeated the ritual with the other breast, and she whispered, "Meeks, please... I want you now."

"Damn. You're so beautiful," he said, ignoring her plea, lost in his own desire. "I've wanted you for so long."

"Please, baby...please!"

Meeks parted Francine's legs with his knees and slowly entered her, stopping long enough to allow her body to accommodate his size.

* * *

Francine felt complete as she wrapped her legs around his waist, as if a missing part of her was finally being returned. Meeks caressed her face, brushing away tears she hadn't realized she'd shed. He kissed her feverishly as he began to move in and out of her; the natural pace just seemed to set itself. Meeks increased the pressure and the speed, and his rapid movements began to lift Francine off the bed. She wrapped her legs tighter around his waist.

Francine knew her enthusiastic responses to his actions made Meeks want to please her that much more.

"I adore you…and now, you're finally mine," Meeks said as he stared into Francine's eyes. He thrust deeply, and her body trembled with another orgasm. Meeks stayed with her, slowing his pace until she had another before he finally took his own release, fast and hard, a climax so intense he was making sounds that might've been foreign even to him.

Francine dropped her legs, and Meeks joined her on the bed where they both lay spent and breathing hard.

"You all right, baby? I was a little focused there at the end."

"Yes…you…were," she said, still trying to catch her breath. "Talk about a man on a mission."

They both laughed. "Yeah…sorry about that. I'd planned something a little more slow and romantic for tonight—a little less passion," Meeks said.

"Why, afraid I'd think you only wanted me for my body?" Francine asked.

"Exactly," Meeks said, smiling. "But when you walked through my door, everything seemed to disappear from my mind. I just couldn't help myself." Meeks rolled to his side and sat up on his elbow. "I wasn't sure I'd make it through dinner. I knew I had to have you."

Francine smiled up at him. "You're amazing, you know that?"

"So you say. I'll be right back after I take care of this," he said, gesturing at the condom.

Meeks returned to the bedroom to find that Francine had moved up on the bed and was lying on her stomach, half covered with the sheet, hugging the pillow and facing him. While she had the look of a very satisfied woman, she also looked like a woman in love. Her eyes were shuttered closed and Meeks wondered if the love he was seeing was real or wishful thinking. He definitely needed to find out.

He lay next to Francine and kissed her lightly on the lips. A slow, lazy smile spread across her face while her eyes remained closed. Meeks released a satisfied sigh, closed his eyes and joined Francine in his own blissful sleep.

Chapter 18

After thirty minutes in the shower with Meeks, experiencing the most sensual body wash and shampoo of her life—she just knew the man had magical hands—Francine dried herself off, wrapped her hair in a towel and dressed in one of his T-shirts. She laughed at the fact that she now had to go commando because Meeks had wanted her so bad that he'd ripped her panties right off. The thought sent another tingle down her spine.

Francine made her way from the bedroom and into the kitchen.

"Morning," she said, smiling at the sight before her.

Meeks had left the shower first to get breakfast started. Dressed in low-riding drawstring sweatpants and a white T-shirt, he was standing over the stove scrambling eggs.

"Have a seat, beautiful. I have everything under control," Meeks said. He reached for the carafe of juice he'd already pulled out of the refrigerator and filled two glasses.

"I can see that," she said, taking a seat at the bar. "I feel weird sitting here with no underwear on, thanks to you."

Meeks's eyes twinkled with mischief. A wicked smile spread across his face, and his gaze lowered to her thighs.

Francine slowly shook her head. "Don't even think about it."

Meeks laughed, handed a glass to Francine and raised his. "To us."

She raised her glass and nodded her salute before taking a sip.

They spent the next thirty minutes enjoying breakfast while discussing the latest political hot topics and debating the need for so many of the same type of reality TV shows. After clearing away the dishes and cleaning the kitchen together, Francine and Meeks relaxed on the sofa while searching through the Saturday morning TV cartoon choices.

Meeks sighed with satisfaction. He knew that having Francine with him like this, sharing meals and chores and ultimately ending up in his bed every night, was how he wanted to spend each day moving forward. He'd let nothing, not even her, stop that from happening.

He raised their intertwined hands and kissed them again. "I know this probably isn't the best time to tell you this but…" He paused, weighing his words. "But I love you. Francine, I'm in love with you… I have been since we were kids, and I hope like hell you love me, too."

Francine remained silent, but her whole body began to tremble. She offered a wordless nod because her lips parted, then closed, then parted again.

A wide smile spread across Meeks's face. He pulled his hands free from hers and cupped her face. He used the pads of his thumbs to wipe away tears, then kissed each eye, her nose and her lips. "I'll take that to mean you love me, too," he said, smiling.

"Yes…yes, I love you, too," Francine said after finally finding her voice. Her arms circled his neck, and she kissed him passionately.

Meeks's heart soared at this realization, and in that moment, everything else just seemed to fade away—the past, the fighting and, surprisingly, the job.

He reached in between the sofa's cushions and pulled out two packs of condoms. "Oh, a sofa with its own supply of condoms. *Nice*," Francine said as they both laughed.

In what seemed like one fluid movement Meeks took Francine's shirt off, sat back against the sofa and pulled her leg across his lap so she was straddling him, riding him to a wave of pleasure that went on for what seemed like an eternity.

Only later, when they were sated and she was curled in his arms, did he notice it. "Shit… Francine, the condom broke," Meeks said, his voice slightly higher than normal.

Francine sighed and her eyes widened.

"Look, baby, you don't have anything to worry about. I'm healthy, and I'm sure you are too, so…"

"Yes, I am," Francine said before he could finish his next thought.

"So I guess the only thing we need to worry about is the possibility of pregnancy. That is, unless you're on the pill or something."

"No, not anymore. After I got…hurt…"

"You mean after you got shot," Meeks corrected, frowning.

Francine's whole body tensed at his reaction. It was clear that Meeks was remembering that day. She reached up and smoothed out the lines on his forehead and gave him a quick kiss on his lips.

She watched as his shoulders dropped and his body relaxed.

"I got off track, and since I wasn't seeing anyone…" Francine gave a nonchalant shrug "…I didn't worry about starting up again. It's the wrong time anyway. I'm sure it'll be fine."

"Well, if you're not worried, I'm not worried," Meeks said, staring in her eyes and brushing her hair off her shoulder. "Besides, knocking you up wouldn't upset me in the least…not one bit."

Staying at home barefoot and pregnant, waiting for your man to come home every day, just doesn't seem like it's your style. Jasmine's words echoed in her mind, and for a minute, Francine froze. *You're just as strong and independent as I am. At least, from everything I've heard.* Francine loved Meeks, but she still wasn't ready to give up her whole life for him. They needed to talk.

Meeks started kissing Francine's neck and collarbone, and she knew she had to stop him before she couldn't think, let alone talk. But before she could speak, he took her mouth with such possession that she flowed into him and let him take her on another journey. Important conversations would have to wait.

In fact, serious conversations of any type were put on hold. Spending a quiet weekend with Francine only confirmed to Meeks that he was doing the right thing in regards to how he planned to handle Tiffany's case, as well as get the company out of the celebrity personal protection business. They were an international security firm for Fortune 500 companies around the world that held patents on state-of-the-art security systems. Once their latest patent—based on some of Frank Blake's old designs, which Robert had modernized—was approved, financially, their company would be in another stratosphere. They didn't need to cater to celebrities.

Before he could put his plan into action, Meeks saw Francine crossing the office floor, headed to the agency's elevators and wearing the standard company uniform with her gun belt on her hip, diamond cross necklace around her neck and tracking watch on her wrist. Meeks knew this could only mean that she was planning to go work on Tiffany's case, and he knew he had to put a stop to the nonsense immediately.

He caught up to Francine just before she made it to the elevators.

"Why are you dressed like that?" Meeks asked, frowning and looking her over head to toe. "And where are you going?"

Francine looked around her before responding. "Well, it is Monday morning, and I'm working, hence the outfit," she said through visibly gritted teeth, clearly keeping in mind that they were in a public area as she gestured at her clothes with her hands. "And if you must know, I'm going to Tiffany's place to check on the newly installed security system."

"No, you're not. I thought we cleared this up over breakfast this morning. I'm operations," Meeks said, pointing to himself first and then back to Francine, "and you're administration," he continued sarcastically, not caring about where they stood.

"Like 'you Tarzan, me Jane'?" Francine put her hands on her hips and glared up at him.

"What?"

"Never mind…look, you said I needed to stay away from Tiffany's case and let you handle it, and I disagreed," she clarified, reaching for the down button only to have her target blocked by Meeks's body.

"Cine—"

Francine held up her right hand, then crossed her arms. "We're not doing this again, and we're certainly not doing it here."

Meeks sighed. "Okay, look, we… I know how capable you are, but we have a team of extremely talented people, most of whom you've helped to train and develop, whose sole job is to do what you're about to go do. Hell, we're even stuck with Jasmine, who'd happily take the lead on things. Personal issues aside, she's damn good at her job, and I should know since I was her mentor and even trained her on a few things."

Francine sighed and dropped her arms.

"Why don't we *both* just let them do their jobs while we do ours? Besides, if you have a couple of hours to blow, I can think of a much nicer way to spend it than crawling around in a hot attic checking on a security system we both know was installed correctly." Meeks smiled and winked as he took a couple of steps toward her.

Francine looked around again, as if to confirm that they were providing entertainment for their staff.

"Well, since you put it like that." Francine moved around Meeks and pushed the up button. The doors opened immediately. She walked into the elevator and said, "You coming?"

He smirked and followed behind her. As the doors closed he whispered, "Soon enough."

As soon as the doors reopened to their floor, Meeks exited the elevator carrying Francine. He had them in her apartment, in her bedroom and undressed with him wearing protection in record time. Meeks reached for Francine's ankles and gently pulled her to the edge of the bed. He wrapped her legs around his waist, grabbed her hips and raised her butt up off the bed. In one powerful thrust, he was buried deep inside her. He took her hard and fast; only this time he pulled back before he sent them both over the edge.

"Please, baby... I need...please," Francine cried as her legs tightened around his waist.

"No, baby...not yet. We've only just begun."

"Yes, now! Meeks...please," she cried as she arched her back and swiveled her hips faster and faster. Meeks could see how determined Francine was not only to take her own pleasure again, but to make sure he took his, too.

Surrendering to her will, Meeks followed her lead until finally he couldn't hold himself back any longer. Her inner walls gripped him just before she screamed out his name. He followed with his own release.

Meeks collapsed on top of Francine. "Sorry, Cine," he said between breaths. "You...all right?"

"Sorry? For what?"

"That last time was a little bit...rough," he said as he rolled onto his back.

Francine laughed. "Yeah, I'm fine. You know me, Meeks. I'm not made of glass. I'm pretty strong."

Meeks held her gaze as he marveled at the strength she showed every day, succeeding in a male-dominated field, the fierce way she fought for the things she believed in and the unconditional love she had for her family. He pulled her into his arms. "I know you are," he said as he kissed her temple.

"What time is it?"

Meeks checked his cell phone that was on her nightstand. "Almost noon."

"If we don't get out of this bed, we'll never get anything else done today," Francine said.

"Lunch before we get back to work?" he asked.

"Sure, I'll make a chicken salad. Feel free to shower first."

Meeks gave Francine a quick peck on the lips, got up and made his way to the bathroom.

In the shower, he looked at all the delicate bath products that surrounded him. They all screamed Francine, and he quickly realized that deciding to shower at her place before going to conduct a team meeting with twenty men was a mistake. But leaving now with the scent of sex all over him would be an even bigger one.

Meeks took another look around, opened the door and yelled, "Cine! Do you not have anything in here that doesn't smell like a girl?"

Francine walked into the bathroom laughing. She held out a bar of plain white soap and an unopened shaving kit set. "Here, maybe this would be better," she said, handing him the scent-free soap.

A shaving kit and men's deodorant. "Why do you have these?" he asked.

"This is a leftover from last year's team gift for the guys. If you paid closer attention to what we give out, you'd know that."

"Bless you," Meeks said before giving her a not-so-quick kiss. "Care to join me?" he asked.

Before Francine could respond, Meeks had grabbed a condom from the bathroom drawer, pulled off her robe, drawn her into the shower, propped her against the wall and was inside her.

"But what about lunch?" she protested.

"You *are* lunch!"

Francine held on for the ride as Meeks took the idea of showering together to a whole new level.

Chapter 19

Nearly five weeks had passed and Francine still hadn't had a chance—or more accurately, had not found the nerve—to talk to Meeks about their relationship and where *he* saw things going. There hadn't been any additional word or sightings from Tiffany's stalker since they'd agreed that, because Jasmine had been forced on them, they should utilize her skills. They decided to let her and their team take the lead on Tiffany's case. Francine realized that taking a small step back and relinquishing some control didn't mean she was giving up, or worse, giving in. Besides, she knew Farrah would keep her apprised of anything she felt Francine needed to know.

Things had been going so well between Meeks and Francine that she thought maybe she had no reason to be too concerned about his tendency to try to control everything, including her. During the day Meeks tried not to interfere with her work or her schedule, and they spent their evenings together at either his place or hers. Francine was feeling more comfortable with her decision not to have "the talk" with him and dissect their relationship. That is, until she read an incident report on Tiffany's case that she had never seen before.

The phrase that most stood out to her in the report read: "Still no sign of Jergens, but extra security for the photo shoot is in place. Blood on flowers confirmed to be that of suspect Lee Jergens, as were the prints on the bottle of perfume."

"What the hell?" she said, scanning the document a second time.

Francine looked at the report again and realized that the incident report was sent to her in error. It was meant for Meeks's eyes only. This was a follow-up to several others that he'd already received and failed to mention to her.

"Damn you, Meeks!" Francine yelled. She picked up her phone and dialed her sister. "Farrah, can you step into my office when you get a second?"

Francine sat, drumming her fingers on her desk, as she waited for her sister's response.

"Sure, I'll be there in a few. You okay?" Farrah asked.

"No... I'm not okay," Francine said and disconnected the call. "So much for not interfering in my work," she said as she reread the report.

Francine turned to her computer and after doing a little digging, she retrieved all the reports she'd obviously missed from the company's central database and began to read. The most surprising and hurtful thing was the fact that Meeks was still on the case. He was leading things from afar.

Francine looked up the moment Farrah walked in. Farrah froze when she saw the priority case file on Francine's desk and quickly shifted her gaze to the floor before turning to close the door. That was all the confirmation Francine needed. Her sister was also in on the plan to keep her out of the loop.

Farrah sat in the chair across from her sister's desk. "What's up, Cine?" she asked, crossing her legs and resting her forearms on the chair.

Francine leaned forward in her chair with her hands laced together on her desk and glared at her sister. "What's up? *What's up*?" she echoed. "Why don't you tell me what's up?"

"Obviously, by the look of things," Farrah said, gesturing toward the file lying open on the desk, "you're up to speed."

"Not for everything," Francine snapped. "How could you do this? Keeping me in the dark, allowing everybody else to do the same?" She gestured to her sister, then herself, and said, "We're a team…you, me and Felicia. How could you allow this to happen?"

The sisters just stared at each other, and after several moments of tense silence, Farrah pushed out a slow breath, and Francine relaxed back into her chair.

"Look, Cine, I'm sorry but Meeks is scared to death something bad is going to happen to you. Add that to the possibility of a baby—"

"Baby! What baby?" Francine asked, holding up her hands as though she was being arrested.

"*Your* baby," Farrah said, frowning and tilting her head to the side. "I couldn't help but go along with Meeks."

"I'm not having a baby…well, not yet, I don't think." She sighed and looked at her sister. "Just tell me what you're talking about."

"Meeks said that there was a good chance that you could be pregnant," Farrah answered. "And he already didn't want you in any danger or getting overtired, especially after that last incident."

"And you didn't think to ask me?" Francine asked, shaking her head. "Farrah, you know how he can be."

Farrah folded her arms across her chest. "Yes, and I also know how you can be."

Francine sat up straighter in her chair and mirrored her sister's actions. "What's that supposed to mean?"

"You put everything and everyone before yourself, and I wasn't willing to take any chances with my niece or nephew," Farrah explained with a touch of anger in her voice.

"Okay, first of all, I'm pretty sure I'm not pregnant."

Farrah dropped her arms. "Just pretty sure? Did you take a test, see a doctor?"

"No, but I got my period." Francine frowned and diverted her eyes away from her sister.

"Look, that's all beside the point—"

Farrah rolled her eyes, raised both hands and sat back in her chair. Her frustration was clear.

"You all had no right keeping me out of this. This was my case, and the only reason I agreed to step aside was because Meeks convinced me that we *both* needed to step aside, take time together to figure things out, focus on us as a couple…together. So he said he turned the entire case over to Jasmine. Our team reports to her and *she* reports to him…to him. He lied to me!"

"No, he didn't," Farrah defended. "You two did need time together, and we've made sure you did—"

"Yeah, by keeping me in the dark, yet keeping Meeks up to speed and involved," she complained. "You're my sister. You're supposed to be on my side."

"I am, damn it, and you know it!" Farrah sprang forward so forcefully she nearly fell out of her chair. "Always have been…always will be—even when you're wrong."

The sisters stared at each other for several moments before simultaneously saying, "I'm sorry."

They both smiled, and Farrah sat back in her chair.

"Look, Francine, Meeks loves you like crazy," Farrah said, adjusting the ponytail that sat high on her head. "The thought of you being in danger, especially if you're pregnant, would drive him insane. And that would drive us all insane. I didn't think keeping you out of this one case would be that big of a deal."

"I know he does, and I love him like crazy, too. But don't you see why this is a big deal?" Francine asked, as she rose from her desk and walked over to her mini refrigerator where she removed two bottles of water. "Want one?"

"No, thanks," Farrah answered.

Francine took several sips from her bottle, trying to fight a sudden wave of nausea. As she returned to her chair, the doorknob rattled, and her attention focused there as she said to her sister, "Meeks can't think he can just step in and dictate my life, even if I'm pregnant."

Meeks opened the door and walked into Francine's office just in time to hear her declaration.

"Is that so?" he asked. The door swung open and he strode into the office.

Meeks stood inside the doorway dressed in the company T-shirt, which showed off those broad shoulders and arm muscles, along with black jeans that accentuated his very fine butt, with his hands on his hips, a deep frown on his face and a clenched jaw. Meeks's glare moved between Francine's face and the papers on her desk. "So I see you've been doing a little light reading."

"That I have," Francine said, standing and crossing her arms.

The room remained quiet for several moments before

Farrah broke the silence. "Well, it looks like you two have a few things to discuss, so if you'll excuse me…" She hurried toward the door but glanced back over her left shoulder at her sister. Farrah leaned in to Meeks and whispered something that Francine couldn't quite catch, and then rushed out the door.

"So, care to explain to me what the hell you think you were doing taking over my case and leaving me out of the loop?"

"First things first. Tell me, *are you pregnant*?" Meeks asked with what looked like a glimmer of hope in his eyes.

Francine sighed, realizing that her sister had given Meeks all the ammunition he needed to push the issue. "No…maybe… I don't know," she said, frowning as she realized that she should be more sure of what was going on with her own body.

"What the hell does that mean, Cine?"

"It means I had an unusual cycle this time. It means I've been too scared to take a test or go see my doctor. That's what it means, okay?"

Meeks crossed the distance between them. "Baby, we have to find out."

"Don't 'baby' me, mister! And why?" she challenged, brushing off his attempt to take her into his arms. "So you can have an official reason to try to control my life?"

"That's not fair. I'm not trying to run your life, Cine," Meeks defended himself.

"Oh, really?" Francine put her hands on her hips and glared up at him. "What do you call it then?"

"I call it trying to protect you—"

"From what?"

"From yourself!" Meeks snapped, matching her stance. "I'm going to do everything in my power to keep you and our baby safe."

She released a deep sigh and went to the window. "Baby or no baby, Meeks, you have no right to try to control my life."

Meeks closed the distance between them, snaked his arms around Francine's waist and pulled her into his chest. She gave no resistance.

"I have every right to protect the love of my life who could very well be carrying my child. Not to mention my future wife," he whispered into her ear before turning her around to face him.

Francine felt the tears begin to pool in her eyes as she saw Meeks looking down at her with an expression so loving it made her heart ache. "Is that supposed to be some sort of proposal?" she asked, smiling up at him.

"No, just a statement of fact," Meeks said, lowering his head to claim her lips in a passionate kiss that set her body on fire.

Arrogant ass. Francine shook her head.

"All right, I get you want to protect me, and I think it's sweet—in an overbearing caveman sort of way," she said, giving him a warm smile.

"Francine." He leaned his forehead against hers. "I'm only—"

"Wait, Meeks, let me finish." Francine placed her finger over his mouth. "I know you want to protect me, and it makes me love you even more. But baby, you have to understand, I have a job to do just like you—a job I'm very capable of doing with or without you by my side, and one that I've worked hard to prove that I deserved."

"I know you have, Cine, but I think you're confused about your job description."

"What are you talking about?" Francine asked, pushing out of his hold and stepping away from him.

"You're CEO of one of the most successful security

firms in the country. You're not a full-time agent any longer, Cine, and it's about time you stopped acting like it and started acting like an executive," he said, shoving his hands in his pockets.

"I've always done *both* jobs, and you know it," she said, pointing her finger at him.

"No, get it right!" he countered. "First you were hired as an agent, and then you were promoted to CEO. You created this hybrid role."

"So?"

"So," Meeks snapped, "look where it's gotten you lately."

"What are you talking about? I'm damn good at both jobs, and you know it," she said.

"No, I don't." Meeks said as he removed his hands from his pockets, checked and adjusted his watch. "You're an excellent CEO, and you *were* an excellent agent, but you can't be excellent at both at the same time."

"The hell I can't!" she protested. "I'm just as capable as you are at getting things done and even kicking a little ass if I have to. Don't ever forget that either," Francine said, poking her index finger in his chest.

He caught her finger in his hand. "I know how capable you are, Cine, but that won't stop me from trying to keep you safe or from taking unnecessary risks, *especially* if there's a baby coming. It's not fair to our child to put both its parents in danger."

"Then why don't *you* stop working in the field, Mr. COO?" she asked, tilting her head.

"Don't be ridiculous!"

"Oh, now I'm ridiculous?" she said, throwing her hands in the air.

"Yes, because my job requires me to be in the field from time to time and you know it." Meeks walked over to her bookshelf and removed one of her reference guides. "That's why your father created the position years ago, so that he and my father could share the workload. My father took care of the field operations, and your father handled the sales and administration side of things, just like we *should be* doing it today. You're the one who decided to dip those beautiful toes of yours into *my* side of the game."

"Is that what this is really all about…me stepping on your toes?" she asked.

"You know damn well it's not," Meeks said, looking up from his book. "We're not talking about this anymore. You're off this case, and you're staying off."

"Like hell I am," she shot back. "You have no right to make such a declaration!"

With a slight curve of his mouth he said, "I thought we covered my rights already. Now you answer this question—when are you going to find out if we're pregnant?"

Francine glared at Meeks. She knew she should tell him what she already suspected. She didn't need a test to tell her what she already knew in her heart. Farrah was right: the triplets' cycles had always been like clockwork. If being late wasn't enough to convince her she was carrying Meeks's child, her extremely tender breasts and this morning's brief bouts of nausea were. Sharing these symptoms with Meeks was reasonable, but Francine wasn't in any mood to be reasonable.

"I'll schedule a doctor's appointment sometime next week," she snapped.

"Next week? Why don't you take one of those over-the-counter tests?" he asked, his voice laced with excitement and confusion.

"Because a blood test is more accurate this early in a pregnancy. Besides, what's the hurry? It's not like it will change anything right away if I am…not really."

Meeks frowned down at Francine. "You really have lost your mind if you think things aren't going to change if you're pregnant."

"Don't try to put your demons on me," Francine warned.

Meeks froze and raised his chin. "I don't have—"

"Yes, you do," Francine said, putting up her right hand to stop his protest. "I'm not reckless or needy, and I never put myself before others and their safety. The devil will repent before I risk hurting my own child."

Meeks recoiled back as though he'd been hit. Multiple memories flooded his mind: losing his father as a young man, his inability to recognize Jasmine's dangerous ambition and her sometimes thoughtless behavior when he'd first started working with her, which had put lives in jeopardy, and Francine's injury. These were the very demons he tried to deny.

"I know that, Francine," he said softly. "I know you would never do anything to put others in danger. What I'm more worried about is you putting yourself in danger. It's my job as head of the family—"

"Head of what family?"

"Our family, Cine," he said, pointing his finger between the two of them. "And don't you dare say we're not a family."

"Meeks, this isn't the '50s, you know. Pregnant women… wives, do work. Many of them run companies, run in marathons and lift weights. And yes, some even fight the bad guys."

Meeks walked slowly toward Francine, setting the reference book down on her desk, and stared down at her. Francine stood her ground and raised her chin in a defiant manner. "My woman…my wife will not put herself in unnecessary danger. And let me make myself perfectly clear. You will be my wife."

Meeks turned on his heel and walked out of Francine's office.

"Again, if that's your idea of a proposal, it sucks!" she shouted after him.

Chapter 20

Meeks was too furious to return to his office, so he headed down to the gym. When he finished a grueling seven rounds in the ring with his trainer and thirty more painstaking minutes on the bag, every muscle in his body was screaming. The last thing Meeks wanted to deal with was the leggy redhead walking his way wearing an extremely tight red-and-black sports bra with a matching pair of shorts that fit like a glove.

"Jasmine, what are you doing here?" Meeks asked. "And what the hell do you think you're wearing?"

Jasmine arched her back, ensuring that Meeks had a clear view of her breasts, and smiled. "This old thing? It's just a little something I had lying around."

"I thought you were covering Tiffany tonight," Meeks said.

"I switched with that Jenna chick from one of Robert's other teams that wasn't busy, the blonde one that needs to touch up her roots. You remember how much I like to switch things up, don't you?" she asked, giving him a sexy smile.

Meeks glared at Jasmine and said nothing.

"Tiffany is on a play date with one of her friends, shopping or something," she said, waving her hands in a dismissive manner. "Since there hasn't been anything new from Jergens, I thought I'd come work off a little extra energy. I was hoping to find someone to work out with. Interested?" she asked, giving him a flirtatious smile.

"Not wearing that, you're not," he said, frowning. "We have a dress code that *everyone* adheres to, and that includes workout clothes that we provide. If you want to work out in this gym, you will, too. Is that clear?"

Jasmine rolled her eyes and pulled her hair into a tight ball at the back of her head. "Even your precious Francine?" she asked.

"Everyone!"

"Fine," she said, raising her hands in a surrendering gesture.

"Get with Mary, and she'll give you a set," Meeks said as he walked toward the door.

"If I go change, will you work out with me then?" she asked, pointing toward multiple weight machines. "I could really use a spotter. You have a state-of-the-art gym here and some of this equipment is unfamiliar to me."

"Sorry, I'm done, and unfortunately, no one else will be around until after six. So if you want to come back then, you're more than welcome as long as you're appropriately dressed."

She folded her arms and said, "Let me guess, a long dress with a chastity belt?"

"Nothing so drastic. I'm sure you'll approve." Meeks gave Jasmine a small nod and left the room.

* * *

Francine had given up trying to get any more work done. She made a quick stop at the convenience store and went back to her apartment. She changed out of work clothes and into a white T-shirt, blue jean overalls and steel-toe boots—clothes more appropriate for her workshop. When Francine had first built out her apartment, she made two of her bedrooms smaller than the original plans had called for in order to create a space that she considered a retreat. The rustic feel and smell of the different woods were the perfect cure to a difficult day.

Francine unlocked the oversize steel door she had installed to help soundproof the room and keep unwanted smells from her work away from the rest of her place. She pushed open the door, exposing the open space with hardwood floors, floor-to-ceiling sliding glass doors, and two twelve-foot work tables standing five feet apart in the middle of the room. Multiple storage units throughout held different types of wood and woodworking equipment. Two unfinished pieces sat on one of the tables, while the other held a door that Francine was refinishing for her baby sister's apartment.

Francine entered her workshop, and an immediate sense of calm came over her body. After closing the door behind her, she opened the glass doors and walked out onto the balcony. She took a deep breath, and as she exhaled, the weight that she'd entered with drifted right over the concrete barrier. Once she returned inside, she put on her protective eye gear and mask. She turned on her electric sander and went to work.

While Francine felt the tension leave her body as she pushed the sander across the wood, she couldn't help but think about her fight with Meeks. She kept replaying their words over and over again in her mind. The one phrase—

you can't be excellent at both—stood out more than any others.

She began to wonder if she really could have it all: the career she loved so much and a family with the man she knew she wouldn't live without. Would she have to give up one for the other? And if she did, would she be happy in the long run, or would she feel resentful in some way? Those were the nagging questions she had, and she knew there was only one person who could help her work through them.

Two hours later, Francine had finished up in her workroom, was fresh out of a long hot shower and dressed in a pair of black-and-white print leggings and white tank top. She'd made herself a sandwich, which she'd eaten, and was now sitting cross-legged on the sofa wrapped in a cashmere throw, nursing a cup of tea.

"You've put this off long enough," Francine said to herself. "If anyone can help you work out this thing, you know she can."

Francine placed the cup on her ottoman, reached for her cell and keyed in a set of familiar numbers. She smiled the minute a voice came through the line.

"Hi, Mom, got a sec?"

"Hello, sweetheart…is everything all right?" Victoria Blake asked.

Francine's smile widened, and she sat farther back into her sofa. She heard the sounds of her mother settling in for the conversation—the water turning off and a chair being dragged across the floor. Her mother always stopped whatever she was doing and took a seat at the kitchen table whenever any one of her daughters needed to talk.

"What makes you think something's wrong?" she said, her voice barely above a whisper. Taking a seat and asking that question meant she was in for a long conversation, whether she needed one or not. Francine almost regretted making the call.

"A mother knows these things, my dear. Now speak up and spit it out," she ordered.

Francine laughed. She always loved her mother's quick wit, sharp tongue and take-no-prisoners attitude. "Well, I've been thinking about my life lately and the choices I've made. And I was wondering if maybe it was time to make some changes. That is, if I'm even capable of making a change."

"What kind of change are you talking about?"

"Oh, I don't know, marriage…a family, maybe," Francine said, trying to keep her voice level.

Several moments of silence ensued before Mrs. Blake asked, "Is there something you want to tell me?"

"No, Mom," she whispered. "I guess I was just wondering if anyone really can have it all. You know, a successful career, a husband…kids."

"Well, your definition of 'having it all' may differ from mine," she answered. "I think I have it all…a wonderful husband, three beautiful daughters, a lovely home, an active charity life and I don't work outside the home."

When her mother said *husband* and *daughters*, there was so much love in her voice it almost brought Francine to tears.

"But didn't you ever want more…a career?"

Francine's mother laughed, and Francine imagined her mother shaking her head like she always did when she thought her daughter wasn't getting something. Her mother sighed and said, "A lot of women have fulfilling careers that take them outside the home. But Cine, raising my children, helping those less fortunate and taking care of your father *is* my career choice."

"And I can sometimes be a handful," Francine heard her father say in the background.

"Sometimes?" her mother challenged. Her question was followed by a hearty laugh and the sound of the phone dropping to the floor.

Francine shifted on her swivel chair, picturing her father tickling and kissing her mother breathless like he always did, and it made her heart swell. The way they expressed their love for each other, regardless of the audience, and stood strong together on just about everything was a sight to behold. It was something that Francine wanted—just not at the cost of all her hard work, all she'd achieved in this male-dominated industry.

Francine heard her mother fumble with the phone after sending her father on his way. "Cine, are you still there?"

"Yes, Mom," she said, laughing.

"Sorry about that," she said, both sighing and laughing. "Crazy man. Anyway, where was I? Oh, yes," then she went on. "I could have continued nursing before and after we married, but when I met your father I knew what I wanted more."

"But that's not for me," Francine said, retrieving her cup of tea. "At least, I don't think it is."

"I wouldn't be so sure," she warned. "I know you want to be just like your father and conquer the international security world and all, but Cine, that doesn't mean you can't be a wife and mother too someday. It's all about compromise and balance."

"Meeks doesn't seem to want to compromise," Francine said in a whispered tone.

"What! You and Meeks…you're seeing each other now?" her mother asked in a highly excited tone.

"Oh, shit!" Francine said, almost spilling the tea. "Did I say that out loud?"

"You most certainly did! And watch your language, young lady," she said.

Francine listened for her father's response. She knew her mother would be excited by the notion of her and Meeks finally getting together, but her father was a different story. His former business partner's son and his daughter? She really didn't know what his reaction would be. While Francine didn't think her father would be too upset—not after all the wonderful things he always had to say about Meeks—she just wasn't ready to have that conversation.

"How long has this been going on?" her mother asked.

"Almost six weeks."

"Well, it's about time," she said. Again, her voice held a world of excitement.

Francine released a quick sigh. "Why does everyone keep saying that?"

"I guess it's because we've all seen what you two have been trying so hard to fight for years. Now what's going on, Cine?"

"Mom, not only does Meeks want us out of the celebrity personal protection business, as you know, but he also wants me to stop working in the field, to stop leading cases."

"And?" her mother asked.

Francine heard the pop of a soda can before her mother said to her husband, "You can only have half of that." Ever since her father recovered from his illness, Francine's mother had been extra careful about everything he ate and drank. She said losing her husband at such a young age was not an option.

Victoria and Frank had been married for thirty-three years after meeting at a nightclub in Spanish Harlem in New York. The only Caucasian girl in a room full of

African-American and Hispanic partygoers, she stood out. From the moment Frank first took her hand and led her to the dance floor, Victoria had known he'd be her husband one day.

At their wedding, Francine's father had promised to love her mother for the rest of her life. And Victoria Blake was not letting him off the hook.

"Mom, I can't let him control me like that."

"Control you?" she said, and let out an exasperated sigh. "Cine, baby, weren't you the one who wanted to step away from fieldwork so you could work more closely with your father on the business end of things, even before he got sick?"

"Yes, but—"

"And didn't you tell me the only reason you took cases for as long as you did was to reassure your father that you understood the business from top to bottom? And to ease his mind when he finally turned the reins over to you?"

"What's your point, Mom?" she said with a little more bite than she intended.

"My point is, young lady," she replied in a tone that didn't hide her irritation, "Meeks asking you to do something you were already planning on doing—for quite some time, mind you—is not trying to control you. And you *know* it." Her tone said that she meant business.

"He didn't exactly *ask*, Mom," she countered. "He basically *told* me what to do."

"You are a grown woman who's more than capable of doing what you think is best for you. Did he give you a reason why he wants you out of the field?"

"Meeks thinks that we shouldn't both be in danger if it's avoidable," she explained, leaving out the rest of his statement—the part where he had added, *Especially if there's a baby coming.*

"I don't see why you think he's trying to control you, Cine," she said. "Yes, he may be doing that thing that men do—trying to protect us when we don't need protection."

"Right!"

"But sweetheart, that's what they *do*," she nearly sang. "They're men. It's their role."

"So what...my role is to stay home and have babies?" she said, laughing, though it truly was no laughing matter to her.

"As a matter of fact, it's a role I cherish, thank you very much," her mother spat back at her.

"Mom, I didn't mean..."

"It's all right, baby. You and your sisters have always been strong and independent, just as your father had always wished you'd be. But I'd always hoped that a little of me would have rubbed off on you, too."

"Oh, Mom, you have," she said, realizing that their entire conversation might have been a shot in the heart to a woman who took great pride in living the type of life that Francine was rejecting. "Where do you think we get our strength, our compassion and our ability to love unconditionally?"

"Sweetheart, if you love Meeks unconditionally, then you'll have to trust it...trust *him*."

Francine snatched a tissue from the box that sat on the side table next to her chair and dabbed at the moisture spilling from her eyes.

"Know that he'd never use that love against you. If you can do that, you two will be able to work things out, no matter how difficult you might think they are. I promise."

"Thanks, Mom," Francine said, trying to hold back the rest of her tears. This was no time for crying! What the hell was wrong with her?

"Mom, I have a favor to ask."

"Okaaay," she drawled.

"Please don't tell Dad about all this. I'm still sorting through things," Francine requested tentatively. "I'll tell him soon… I promise."

Francine knew how much her mother hated keeping things from their father, even if it was for a short period of time, but she knew that she would—for a little while anyway.

"All right, but you have to tell him…and soon," she said.

Francine bid her mother goodbye.

She would find the right time to tell her father, but it could not be right now.

Francine pulled her knees to her chest, wrapped her arms around her legs and laid her head against her knees.

Meeks would never use her love for him against her. And she did love him enough to compromise, but first things first. Francine sat up straight and took a deep breath, trying to hold off another bout of nausea as she made her way to the bathroom. She picked up the package she'd purchased several days before and stared at the label.

She had waited long enough.

Chapter 21

Meeks had arrived at the office early because he hadn't been able to sleep. He hated not speaking to or being with Francine, but he knew she needed space and time to cool down. He couldn't figure out why she couldn't understand his point of view. Didn't she understand that if anything ever happened to her, he'd be lost, too? Meeks wanted to march into her office and demand that she accept the fact that he loved her more than his own life and that he'd never hurt her. But he knew better. He knew she needed to come to terms with things in her own way and at her own pace. He just hoped that it didn't take too long.

"Meeks, man, we need to talk. Now," Robert said as he entered his office.

"What's up?" Meeks asked as Robert stood in front of his desk.

"Have you checked your email yet?" he asked, removing his sunglasses and using them to gesture toward the computer.

"No, why?"

"Pull up the email from Karen. I had her send you some stuff while I was driving in. You won't believe this shit. Thanks to Farrah's leads, I was able to dig deeper into Bluebonnet's financials and Jergens' history, employment, medical, et cetera," Robert said, resting his sunglasses on Meeks's desk and taking a seat.

Meeks read through Robert's reports and looked up at his friend, whose face was twisted in a frown. "Wait, am I reading this right? Lee Jergens was in a mental hospital when most of the attacks occurred against Tiffany? And the flowers with Jergens's blood on them were bought with a Bluebonnet executive credit card in Bill Morgan's name the day before he was released from the hospital."

"Yep, but keep reading. I want you to see it for yourself," Robert said, tilting his head toward the computer.

Meeks put his eyes on the screen. "Is this real? The pictures of the male body parts do, in fact, belong to Lee Jergens. So he was stalking Tiffany."

"Yes," he agreed, "But it seems he wasn't the only one."

"So let me get this straight," Meeks said, sitting back in his chair. "All the names on Tiffany's friends and family list check out. All the men from her Bluebonnet detail check out. The only person with a vendetta and/or obsession for this woman is Jergens. But we can only trace his involvement through pictures that he may or may not have sent to Tiffany himself." Meeks put two fingers to his head and rubbed his temple. "All the actual physical evidence had to be planted since our suspect was locked up in a mental institution at the time they were delivered. And the most damaging piece of evidence, the flowers, was purchased with a credit card that belongs to Bill Morgan. Is that correct?"

"Yep, that just about sums it up," Robert said as he started searching through his electronic tablet.

"And we still can't seem to locate this Lee Jergens. It's like he's fallen off the face of the earth," Meeks said, his eyebrows pulled together in annoyance.

"No, just hiding out real well, but we'll find him," Robert reassured his friend.

"What else have you found out about Bill Morgan? Something's just not right about that relationship," Meeks said, scratching his day-old beard.

Robert widened a page on his tablet and recited from it, "Nothing we didn't already know. Bill Morgan is forty-two years old, married and divorced only once, had control of Tiffany and her assets until last year when she turned twenty-one and gained full control. He has no criminal record. His personal wealth was less than two million until he gained custody of Tiffany. As of last year's taxes, his personal worth is over twenty million."

"Damn, looks like guardianship pays well," he said, sitting up straight and dropping his hand from his head. "We've seen this kind of thing before. It's obvious that Mr. Morgan has been creative with his bookkeeping and financial advice when it came to handling Tiffany's money. Has anything ever been mentioned about anything inappropriate going on between the two of them?"

Robert frowned and leaned forward in the seat. "What? You think he was doing something to her?"

"I'd hate to think so, but something just isn't right there," Meeks said. "Tiffany may not have gotten full control over all of her money until she turned twenty-one, but when she turned eighteen, she gained access to a large portion of it, and she started to have a say in how things went. Bill Morgan could have been using his position to influence her into doing things his way."

"Why don't we just bring him in and *talk* to him? You know we can get the truth out of him," Robert said, laughing. "Our men don't think too highly of guys who take advantage of young girls."

Meeks shook his head. "Have him brought in so we can ask him about these financial discrepancies. That's a good place to start."

Robert sent a text to one of his men.

"In one piece, Robert," Meeks added.

"Of course," Robert said, laughing and keying in that instruction.

Meeks went back to reading over all the information they had on the case. "You know, either Tiffany has two stalkers that are working together or one has some amazing access to Jergens. Because they've managed to get Jergens's prints, his blood and were able to get close enough to take pictures of his private parts. What does that sound like to you?" Meeks asked Robert.

"Like a woman," Robert replied.

"A woman," Meeks agreed, smiling.

"But who?" Robert asked, placing his tablet on Meeks's desk where he started flipping through it.

Meeks matched his posture and did the same. "It's got to be in here somewhere. We just missed it somehow."

"You better call Jeremy and have him order some lunch. We'll be here a while," Robert said. "Chinese."

While he was happy for the distraction, Meeks was ready to put this case to bed. His relationship with Francine would remain on shaky ground until it was.

"Knock, knock. Cine, you here?" Farrah called out as she entered Francine's apartment.

Francine walked out of her bedroom, down the hall and into her kitchen where she found her sister raiding her refrigerator. "Didn't we agree we'd call before we dropped by on each other or used the keys?"

"Yes, and I did, but you didn't answer," Farrah said as she pulled lunch meat, cheese, crackers, mustard and a bottle of water out of her sister's refrigerator.

"So you just let yourself in? Meeks could have been here," she protested.

"But he's not, right?" she said confidently, sitting at her sister's bar with her ingredients laid out in front of her.

"That's beside the point," Francine snapped as she watched her sister make herself a breadless sandwich.

"Well," Farrah replied before she took a bite. "Don't you have any bread around this camp?"

"Don't you have food at your own place?" Francine asked as she started putting away everything that her sister had finished using before sitting on the stool next to her.

"Nope, I haven't had a chance to go to the store. So, you were expecting company?" Farrah asked, smiling while making her eyebrows dance.

"No, but I will be. As soon as I find Meeks," Francine said, trying not to smile but failing miserably.

"He's in his office working on something with Robert," Farrah said, biting into her food.

"What?" Francine asked, drumming her fingers on the counter.

"Not sure. I just got back from meeting with the Timber Group. We were going over the final contracts, and looks like we're a go now that I've clarified our position on a few things. Another happy new client," she said, laughing and giving her sister that wicked "I kicked butt" smile she wore whenever she'd won a hard-fought battle.

"I bet you did," Francine said, shaking her head.

"By the way, why didn't you tell me their company

attorney was so damn fine?" Farrah asked, finishing off her food and bottled water.

Francine shrugged. "He's all right, I guess," she admitted nonchalantly.

Farrah threw her head back and laughed. "Man, you got it bad."

"I know," Francine said, covering her mouth with both hands and laughing with her sister.

"That food hit the spot," Farrah said, leaning back on the stool and placing her arms on the armrest. She crossed her legs and gave Francine a sideways glance. "Did you ever take that pregnancy test? Am I going to be an aunt?"

Francine dropped her hands into her lap and managed to keep herself from releasing a smile that could outshine the sun, although there was a slight curve to her lips. "I think I need to talk to Meeks first," Francine explained to her sister without meeting her gaze.

"Look at me, Francine," her sister ordered in that voice she usually saved for the courtroom.

Francine knew what it meant when her sister used her full first name in that tone, so she pushed out a slow breath and turned in her chair to face Farrah. There was only a small smile, but it was enough.

Farrah started fidgeting in her seat before she finally started jumping up and down, screaming, "I knew it! I… knew it!" She pulled Francine into a hug.

Francine returned the embrace, but quickly broke it off. "Wait a minute, I cannot confirm or deny anything without talking—"

"To your lawyer," she said, dancing around the room. "Which happens to be me."

Both women laughed.

"Look, Farrah, you know I love you, but I have to talk to Meeks before I say anything."

"No problem, Cine. Besides, I already know. I already *knoo-oow*," she sang with a great deal of enthusiasm, but way off key. "Now I know why Felicia called this morning."

"Felicia called? Is everything all right?" Francine asked.

"Yeah, she was just checking in. You know our baby sister. She had another one of her 'feelings,'" Farrah said, using air quotes to emphasize her point as she sat back down. "You know she calls whenever she can't explain her feelings away. Even after I reassured her that everything was fine, she was still ready to jump on a plane. It took Mom and Dad reminding her how important her research was before she finally calmed down. At least now we know why she had that feeling."

Francine smiled at her sister as she fought the urge to place a hand on her stomach. Instead she swept her hair to the side and started braiding it—anything to keep her hands busy.

"Do we know what Felicia's working on now?" Francine asked.

"No idea. You know how private our baby sister can be," Farrah said, rolling her eyes. "I mean really, how top secret can her medical research be? Maybe she's working on a cure for erectile dysfunction?"

Francine laughed and nodded in agreement.

Farrah stopped laughing and frowned. "Well, now that I think about it, if I was a man and I no longer had use of my—"

"Farrah..." Francine said, giving her sister a disapproving look, preventing her from using the foul language she knew was coming.

"Manhood," Farrah amended, giggling like a schoolgirl. "I'd want to keep it a secret, too."

"Good point," Francine agreed.

"Seriously, maybe our baby sister is working on some new medical breakthrough," Farrah said.

Francine got off the stool and walked to her hall closet where she removed a leather gun belt and strapped it on. She then pulled down her gun from the vault storage that she kept at the top of the closet. After entering her pass code, Francine removed a 9 mm, ensured that it was loaded but that the safety was still on, and then holstered it. After removing a set of handcuffs and clipping them to her belt, she ignored the tracking watch and grabbed two additional ammunition clips before returning the vault to the top of the closet. She closed the closet door and turned to find her sister glaring at her.

"Where are you going? And why are you dressed like you're going on patrol?" Farrah asked, standing with her hands fisted at her sides and frowning.

"Because I am," Francine said, not understanding her sister's enraged expression. "You act like this is the first time you've seen me get ready to go out on a job."

"Cine, you can't," Farrah demanded. She was obviously horrified. "You have to think about the baby."

Francine rolled her eyes. "Calm down, Farrah, it's not what you think," she said as she walked around her sister and back into the kitchen where she'd left her purse.

Francine opened her bag and retrieved the diamond cross necklace that she wore most days but especially whenever she worked in the field. It always made her feel safe. Each sister had one, given to them by their mother for their birthday several years ago. Francine pulled it over her neck before turning to face her sister who had followed her into the kitchen.

"I told Roger I'd cover the meal breaks for the teams at the Weinberg School and the Buffalo Soldiers Museum.

You can't get any tamer than that," she said, shrugging. "Hell, I wouldn't wear all this crap if it wasn't required."

Farrah laughed. "Yeah, you're right about that. Not much happening at a private school where most of the folks are out on break."

"True, or a museum that's not even opened yet," Francine added, laughing and shaking her head. "Sometimes I think, excluding the pro bono work we do, even with the deep discounts we give some companies, we're the ones robbing them with the fees we charge."

Farrah's inner attorney took over. "I object! We are in line with industry standards for the services we provide. Most insurance companies request the level of security necessary to ensure their coverage."

"Hold on, Perry Mason," Francine said, raising both hands, giving her a wide smile. "I was just kidding. Man… your inner lawyer is on point today."

"Sorry about that. The attorney in me really does take over with even the hint of impropriety. How'd you pull such a luxurious duty anyway?" Farrah asked as she pulled out a bottle of Coke from the refrigerator.

"I was in the break room when Roger got a call about his kid getting sick, so I told him to go home and that I'd cover his last stops of the day. It shouldn't take more than a couple of hours," she explained.

"Yeah, but you know Robert can get someone to cover it, Ms. CEO. Excuse me, Ms. *Pregnant* CEO," Farrah said as she raised her left eyebrow.

Francine laughed. "I know, but there isn't anything safer. And the museum is down the street from Jamaica House."

"So you're picking up dinner from Meeks's favorite place. Will you get me my usual order too while you're there?" she asked, pulling a fifty-dollar bill from her pocket. "This is all I have on me."

"Sure."

"Planning a special evening... I wonder why," Farrah teased as she danced around in Francine's kitchen.

Both sisters laughed.

"So no more worries about Meeks wanting to control you?" Farrah questioned.

Francine smiled and shook her head. "No. I mean, I'm starting to see things from his point of view," she replied.

"What?" Farrah asked, placing the back of her right hand on her sister's forehead with a look of shock on her face.

Francine swatted the hand away and pulled on her jacket. "Really..."

"I'm just checking to make sure you're feeling all right," she said.

"Don't get me wrong, I'm not ready to walk away from a very profitable piece of our business just because he says so. Besides, I still think providing personal security to those who need it, even celebrities, is the right thing for us to do," Francine said as she placed her left hand over her stomach. "Meeks will always be overprotective and a little overbearing at times, but I know it's coming from a place of love. Besides, he's right. There's no reason for us both to be in the field at the same time. And taking jobs every now and then will be good for me and something he won't object to...much."

"Especially if it's mundane duty like today," Farrah corrected.

"Right," Francine agreed as she gathered up her things to leave.

"If you give me thirty minutes so I can change clothes and move some things around, I can join you," Farrah offered.

"Thanks, but that's not necessary," Francine said as she extended her arms to check out her fingernails. "I think I'll even try to see if I can squeeze in a manicure, too."

"Wow, you're going all out to break the news," Farrah said as she too collected her things to leave.

"What news?" Francine asked, giving her a sly wink.

The sisters laughed as they embraced before leaving the apartment together.

Chapter 22

Meeks walked into the gray, windowless concrete-walled room that the team used for unofficial interrogations, or "information gathering sessions" as Robert liked to call them, and found Bill Morgan sitting facing the door, nursing a cup of coffee. The well-dressed, physically fit man they'd met several weeks ago looked tired and older than his forty-two years.

Morgan fiddled with his watch a moment before pulling at the neck of the crisp white shirt that complemented his gray pinstriped suit. When Meeks laid eyes on the man's hands, Morgan shifted them under the table, evidently trying to hide a nervous tremor.

Robert followed Meeks into the room, closed the door and leaned against it with his arms crossed in front of him at his waist.

"Mr. Morgan, thanks for joining us," Meeks said, as he took a seat across from him.

"It's not like I was given much choice," he said, rubbing his right forearm and giving Robert an accusatory look.

Meeks looked over his shoulder and glared at his friend.

Robert shrugged. "What? He's in one piece, isn't he?"

Meeks sighed and turned to face Bill Morgan. "Mr. Morgan, do you know why we've asked you here?"

Morgan rose slightly out of his chair and leaned forward, placing his fisted hands on the table. "No…and like I said, I wasn't given a choice," he said with more force behind his words.

Meeks leaned back into his chair and placed his long right leg on the table. He pulled out his cell phone and started checking the messages. "Well, you'll be here for a minute while we convince Tiffany to file embezzlement charges against you," Meeks said, ignoring Mr. Morgan's posturing.

"Embezzlement charges," he said, frowning and dropping back down into his chair.

"Yes," Robert said, finally chiming in but not moving from his spot against the door. "Over the years, how much *have* you stolen from Tiffany—seven…ten million dollars?"

"It's amazing how much this man can dig up when he's motivated," Meeks said, gesturing toward Robert.

"I don't know what you're talking about," Mr. Morgan claimed, though his face had reddened considerably.

"Sure you do, but we're not the ones you need to convince," Meeks said, never taking his eyes off the screen.

"No, that would be a judge and twelve jurors," Robert added, giving Mr. Morgan a small smirk.

Meeks placed his phone face down on the table and crossed his arms. "We're just trying to figure out if you're going to take the weight for the stalking as well, or if you're smart enough to cut a deal."

"Wait…what?" Mr. Morgan said, his round, red face pulled into a mask of confusion.

"Jergens had a partner," Robert said.

"At the time many of the stalking incidents took place, Jergens was actually locked down in a mental hospital," Meeks explained. "So he had to have had inside help."

"And you think it's me?" Mr. Morgan asked, his voice raising a couple of octaves.

"If it's not you, then you know who it is," Meeks said, tilting his head to one side.

"My question is, why? Why would you steal from someone you basically raised?" Robert asked, pushing off the door with his elbows, walking forward and looking down on Mr. Morgan. "Did she reject you or something?"

"Re-reject me," he stammered. "What? Wait, you think there's something going on between me and Tiffany?" he asked with one eyebrow raised.

"I don't really know, but I think you'd like there to be. Did you do anything about those feelings?" Meeks asked, narrowing his eyes.

Mr. Morgan stood and yelled, "Of course not!"

"Sit down!" Robert said as he pushed Mr. Morgan back into the chair.

Robert had used a tone that had Meeks on his feet in seconds. Meeks knew his friend. Hurting women and children was something neither he nor Robert could ever abide, but they needed proof before Meeks could allow any action to be taken. Unfortunately, Robert was more the act-now-ask-questions-later type, which was why Meeks stood behind him—just in case he needed to stop him from pulling Mr. Morgan from his chair by his tie.

"But you do have a thing for her. So much so that you wanted to scare her in hopes that she would…what?" Robert asked, hovering over Mr. Morgan. "Come running into your waiting arms?"

"No! You've got it all wrong," he said, shaking his head.

Meeks could see both fear and confusion on Mr. Morgan's face, so he tapped Robert on the shoulder. Robert straightened up, folded his arms and took a couple of steps back. Meeks watched as relief crawled across Mr. Morgan's face. He wasn't sure what to think.

"Okay, tell us about it…all of it," Meeks said, slipping back into the chair he had vacated.

Mr. Morgan released a deep breath. "I never touched Tiffany, and I never stalked her either," he said, glancing at both men. "Yes, I may have made some questionable business decisions and—"

"Questionable?" Robert chirped.

"You think?" Meeks added.

"There may have been deals where I may have benefited more than I should have, but I'd never do anything to hurt Tiffany," Mr. Morgan said, trying to keep his focus on both of the men across from him.

"So you never touched Tiffany? Not even as a child?" Robert asked, clearly needing clarification.

Morgan parted his lips to speak, but Meeks cut in with, "Careful, and don't lie…he'll know. I won't be able to stop him if you do." Meeks's eyes darted between Mr. Morgan and Robert.

"Of course not," Morgan conceded. "I was her guardian, and I've always looked at her in that way only. That is, until about a year ago when…"

"When she came into all that money," Robert said.

"It wasn't like that," he confessed, focusing his attention on Meeks. "We celebrated her twenty-first birthday, and I suddenly saw her as the beautiful young woman she was…"

"Sure you did," Robert murmured.

"It's true," he protested, but his tone was low, almost weary. "But I knew she'd never see me in that same light, so I kept my feelings to myself."

"You need to do a better job than that," Robert huffed, walking and standing behind Mr. Morgan's chair.

"Tell us about the stalker," Meeks said, giving Robert a silencing look.

"I already told you, I didn't know who the stalker was until you told me, and I have no idea who his partner is," Mr. Morgan insisted, banging his right fist on the table.

"All right, let's talk about all the money you've embezzled from Tiffany and your connection with Bluebonnet."

Morgan took a deep breath, but Meeks raised his hand to stop the denial he knew was coming. "And before you start professing your innocence, we already know you're a partial owner in Bluebonnet—a partnership you bought into by using money you stole from several of Tiffany's accounts. A partnership that came with a lot of perks—a monthly consulting fee, for what exactly I don't know, an expense account and company credit cards."

Mr. Morgan sighed. "I can explain—"

Robert bent forward. "And we can't wait to hear it," he said sourly. "But what we don't understand is why you would trust them with Tiffany's security without disclosing your connection to Tiffany to the company. It's a clear conflict of interest. I mean, I can see how you couldn't share how you paid for the partnership, but damn, man, we're talking about the woman's security. Shouldn't she be able to make an informed decision about who's protecting her?"

Morgan's eyes widened to the size of plates. "Bluebonnet... what do they have to do with Tiffany's stalker?"

"Everything," Robert replied. "We think the stalking started there, especially since a major piece of evidence we were able to uncover was bought with one of their corporate cards. A card assigned to you—"

"What…one of *my* cards was used?" Bill Morgan said, shaking his head in clear disbelief.

"Yes and for some reason, as good as Bluebonnet is, they couldn't figure out what was going on or find the person behind it." Robert stood up straight and crossed his arms as he sat on the edge of the table. "At least that's what they claimed. Yet it only took us a single day of research and a few phone calls to find out about Jergens." His lips spread into a wide smile. "I know we're good and all, but the breadcrumbs that Tiffany's stalkers left were easy to find and even easier to follow."

"Which makes us wonder why they couldn't, or should I say *wouldn't*, resolve this issue a long time ago. There has to be a reason why," Meeks explained.

"I didn't think…" Mr. Morgan said.

"No, you didn't," Meeks said, not letting the man's remorsefulness derail him.

"I don't understand. My relationship with Bluebonnet is a business one. I didn't think it was that big of a deal… what I did. That is until…" Mr. Morgan said before falling silent.

"Until what?" Meeks and Robert asked simultaneously.

"Until the blackmail started," he explained.

Meeks and Robert looked at each other for a moment before focusing on Morgan once again. "That's the ten-thousand-dollar-a-month payment you've been making to some mysterious shell company," Meeks said more as a statement than a question.

Mr. Morgan slowly nodded. "I've been making the payments for the last two years."

"Damn, man," Robert said, crossing his arms. "What did they threaten you with?"

"Everything. Somehow they found out about my relationship with Bluebonnet and that I borrowed money from Tiffany for the buy-in."

"*Borrowed,*" Robert sneered. He stood and walked to the other side of the room.

"This can't just be about your relationship with Bluebonnet," Meeks said.

Mr. Morgan sighed.

"I may have *borrowed* more money from Tiffany's trust fund a little more often than even I want to admit. I set up a few dummy accounts and funneled the money through them. I told myself that it was just a way to better track the money I needed to pay back."

"How were you contacted?" Meeks asked.

"A woman called me—"

"Wait, a *woman* called you?" Meeks asked, leaning forward slightly and noticing the slight shift in Robert's stance. "How do you know it was a woman? Her voice wasn't disguised?"

"It was, but I'm still pretty sure it was a woman," Mr. Morgan said with certainty in his voice.

Robert dropped his arms and stepped closer to the table. "How?"

"It was something she said the first time she called. It was right after Tiffany's twentieth birthday." Mr. Morgan brushed the back of his hand across his forehead. "I took her on a top-secret luxury shopping spree as a gift. It was something we used to do when she was younger whenever she achieved a goal. The caller said they'd hate to have to tell Tiffany that the luxury shopping spree that I had just taken her on to buy all those pairs of Christian Louboutin shoes, Prada bags and that Ralph Lauren luggage that wasn't even in season yet was financed with her own money." He looked Meeks directly in the eye. "Money I stole from her."

"Christian who?" Robert asked, frowning.

"Exactly," Mr. Morgan said, shifting his gaze to Robert. "Not many men know women's fashion by brand. I certainly don't, so I figured it had to be a woman."

"It tells us more than that. It tells us that the blackmailer was close," Meeks explained.

"How so?" Mr. Morgan asked.

Robert checked his watch. "You said it was a top-secret shopping spree."

"Who knew about this shopping trip?" Meeks asked.

"Just me and Tiffany…" Then he shrugged. "And of course her security person."

Robert shared a speaking glance with Meeks. "Was the security person from Bluebonnet?"

"No," he answered, frowning at both men. "You know her. Jasmine Black."

Chapter 23

Francine made her way through downtown Houston and was heading toward the Museum District when she received a call from a private detective-turned-lawyer they often used when they didn't want their agency publicly involved, usually for personal activities. Francine activated her Bluetooth when she read the name on her car's video screen.

"Fletcher Scott, that was fast. Tell me you found something," Francine said.

"I found something, but you knew I would," he replied in that arrogant Southern drawl of his.

"Yes!" Francine said, hitting the side of her steering wheel with the palm of her hand.

"I still don't get why you outsourced this job to me. Why not have your own people handle this, or your sister, for that matter?" Fletcher questioned.

Francine sighed. "I told you, it's a sensitive matter for

all those concerned. So, what did you find out?" Francine asked.

"All right, little lady, your call. Now I went over all the material you sent me and made a few phone calls. The board's bylaws and policies and the company's rules of conservatorship are clear. Even during your dad's recovery period, he was still considered incapacitated. As such, he could no longer act as conservator of his assigned proxies, so his conservatorship was transferred to his executor, and he was never reinstated as required."

Francine stopped at a light and smiled at the crossing pedestrians. "English, Fletcher. I'm the triplet that *didn't* go to law school," she said to her screen as though she was looking into Fletcher's face.

"Oh, sorry. In a nutshell, when your dad got sick, he lost control over his proxies, and according to your company's rules, that control went to his executor, which is—"

"Me," Francine said as she continued through the intersection.

"Yes. I was surprised by that. I would have thought it would have been your mother."

"They made me their executor several years ago. Both my parents said that they knew if the time came, they would never be able to make rational decisions about anything when it came to their other half," she explained.

"So since your father never reinstated his conservatorship, and the proxies weren't revoked, you still have control of them."

Francine pulled her car into an open parking spot she found. "Let me make sure I understand what you're telling me. Because Dad got sick, he lost control over the three proxies he had, and because he didn't have them reinstated, I have control over them."

"Yep…basically that's it," he said.

"Wow, I never realized…"

"Well, you have all the power now, that is, until your dad finally realizes what he needs to do to change things. You know…you *could* use this time to convince those board members to leave their proxies in your hands."

Francine laughed. "Thanks, Fletcher. Send your report and bill to my personal email address," she said.

"Will do, and when you see Robert, tell him to give me a call. I've tried to reach him but you know he stays on the move."

Francine laughed and promised to pass on the message before she disconnected the call and pulled back into traffic.

"Well, well. I told you, Dad, don't count those chickens."

"Say that again," Meeks said, slowly rising from his chair.

"Jasmine Black was the security person we had with us on the shopping spree," Mr. Morgan explained. "She's been our freelance expert for a couple of years now."

Meeks and Robert exchanged a look that caught Mr. Morgan's attention.

"What?" Morgan asked with wide eyes.

"We thought this was the first time that Jasmine worked for you," Meeks explained.

"No, that's why the studio invited her to be on the team. They know her, too," Mr. Morgan said.

"Invited," Robert murmured to himself. "Why didn't this come up before?"

"Because Tiffany thinks of Jasmine as more of a friend than security," he said.

"Excuse us for a moment, Mr. Morgan," Meeks said as he gestured with his head for Robert to follow him.

Both men exited the room and moved into the hall, where Meeks began to pace.

"What's up?" Robert asked, reaching out to stop his friend before he could make another lap.

"Something's not right. Jasmine told me that this was her first gig with Tiffany. She lied to me. But why?"

Robert shrugged. "Maybe she just didn't want you in her business. You know how she is when it comes to that kind of thing. She damn near took your head off a couple of years ago when you offered her the seed money for her company, remember? She couldn't accept you were just trying to be a good friend. You'd swear you were offering her money for something other than getting her business off the ground."

Meeks shook his head. "Right, I do know her. Think about it, man. Jasmine started working for Tiffany and her management company two years ago, and she had access to all the information she needed to blackmail Bill Morgan. We both know she's smart enough and has all the contacts necessary to figure out who was stalking Tiffany and use it to her advantage. She's an expert pickpocket so she could have easily lifted his credit cards."

"But why? The quarter of a million dollars in blackmail money? She's smarter than that," Robert said, shaking his head. "Besides, rumor has it she makes that on just one of her maintenance gigs."

Meeks held up his right index finger and shook his head and said, "Not two years ago, she didn't."

"So you think that she wouldn't take the money from you to start up her business, but she'd commit *blackmail* to get it?" Robert questioned.

"Yes, I do!" Meeks declared.

"Yeah, but still…if she's behind this, there's got to be another reason," Robert agreed.

Both men walked back into the room to find that Morgan had removed his jacket and was now leaning against the wall.

"Mr. Morgan, you haven't made a blackmail payment in the last two months. Why?" Meeks asked.

Mr. Morgan straitened to his full height. "I got a call from the same woman as before." He walked back to the chair and gripped its back with both hands. "Well, I assumed it was the same woman, and she said I was done, that I didn't need to make any more payments. She said that she'd keep my secret, but that I really should think about keeping my hands out of the cookie jar. She said I'd never hear from her again, and I haven't."

"Just like that and you're done?" Robert questioned with a snap of his fingers.

"What did she say...*exactly*?" Meeks asked.

"That was it." Mr. Morgan frowned and squinted. "Wait, there was more. She said something to the effect of, I should consider all the money severance that had been paid in full."

Meeks's head jerked back, and his forehead creased. He took a couple of steps back as his mind traveled back in time. Mr. Morgan's words took Meeks back to the last time he'd heard similar words.

Meeks had already ended his relationship with Jasmine when she had shown up to one of his job sites wearing a low-cut, body-hugging green dress and a pair of black stilettos, claiming that they needed to discuss the lavish Caribbean vacation they'd planned.

So, what should we do about the trip? she had asked, leaning against her silver Mercedes with legs crossed at her ankles.

Why don't you take it? After all, you planned it, Meeks had said.

Yeah, but you paid for it, she'd said, flipping her hair off her shoulders.

It was a gift, Jasmine, Meeks had said as he gave a nod to a couple of his men who had stopped to admire her assets.

Well, I have an idea, she had said as she walked slowly toward him, her voice low and husky. *How about we still go together? You know, friends-with-benefits style*. Jasmine had placed her right hand over his heart.

I don't think so. You go…enjoy yourself, Meeks had replied, unmoved by her voice or her proposal. He'd plucked her fingers from his chest.

Jasmine had thrown her head back and laughed. She'd pushed out a deep breath, stood and walked around to the driver's side of her car. Before she drove away, she'd looked back at him and said, *Oh, well, I guess I should just consider it severance that's been paid in full.*

"What is it?" Robert asked.

His question brought Meeks back to the present, and he walked out into the hall with Robert following close behind.

"What is it?" Robert repeated.

"It's Jasmine," he stated. "That severance crack is one of her favorite lines. Add that to everything else we know and you have—"

"One big coincidence," Robert declared. "But we need proof if we're going to accuse her of being behind all of *this*."

"You're right. Run her financials. I'm sure there's more out there, but first we have to go tell the girls."

Robert gave Meeks a sideways glance and said, "Wow, someone's changing. Usually you'd plow full speed ahead to take care of things first, and tell Francine about it later."

"Yeah, well, the art of compromise is a learned be-havior."

"So I hear," Robert said, laughing as he followed him toward the elevator. "What do you want to do about Old Man Morgan?"

"Have one of the guys take him upstairs to one of the apartments and sit on him until we figure this thing out. Then meet me in Cine's office." Meeks hit the up button.

Chapter 24

Francine arrived at the Buffalo Soldiers National Museum, her last stop of the day, fifteen minutes early. When she had arrived at her prior stop, the Weinberg School, the team informed her that the school's administration had provided them food for both lunch and dinner. With the school closed for break, they were allowed to eat at their stations, so her coverage wasn't needed. However, since she was already there and wasn't due to arrive at the museum for another hour, Francine had stayed to catch up with the team and get their thoughts on the personal security aspect of the business.

Francine laid her head back onto the headrest of her Mini Cooper and closed her eyes. She thought back to the conversation she'd just had with two of the veteran agents on her team, Victor, a tall, fair-skinned man with colorful tattoos traveling down his arms, and Carlos, a Latino man who was a loving husband and father and had been with the firm almost from its inception. Francine was still surprised by their thoughts around personal security and working with celebrity clients.

Ms. Francine, with all due respect, providing security for celebrities is a pain in the ass—excuse my French. They don't follow instructions, and most of them think they're better than everybody around them. It may be the new thing for agencies to do these days, but we've never been ones to follow a trend, Victor had said as he removed his hat and brushed back his sandy brown hair. *I'm sure they bring in the big bucks, too, but—*

That's not who we are, Carlos had said. *Your dad said the security products we developed and sold along with our corporate system-monitored clients allow us to do pro bono work…and that I get. What I don't understand is what these celebrity clients support, or why we need them. Blake & Montgomery has never been all about money.* Carlos had been leaning against the table that sat behind the marble-and-glass security station at the school's front entrance.

Your old man taught us that. We help and protect people and organizations that need and want the help, even if they can't afford it, Victor had explained.

Like this school, Carlos had said, looking around at the shiny marble flooring, wall-to-wall tinted windows and the long hallway that led to lavishly furnished classrooms with the latest technology. *When the church first got the grant to build a school in this up-and-coming neighborhood, they didn't figure on needing any security.*

Yeah, until they had that break-in shortly after opening it, Victor said, swinging his hat around his index finger, which almost made Francine dizzy.

Then they came to us for help, to your dad and Mr. Meeks. Carlos had swallowed hard and cleared his throat. *Now I don't know how much money you could be making from these folks, but it can't be much. But we give them the same top-notch security we give our downtown clients. And they love us for it—the school, the parents and the community. We feel appreciated, and they feel safe.*

And no drama, Victor had said, putting his hat back on his head.

And no drama, Carlos had agreed.

The sound of a roaring engine brought Francine back to the present—in her car in front of the museum. She slowly opened her eyes and released a deep sigh as she sat forward. Francine had expected a little pushback from the elder statesman Carlos, but Victor's words came as a surprise. Francine checked the time on her car's dashboard clock. *So much for being early.*

She grabbed the tablet from the passenger seat to check the name of the agent she was meeting. "Jimmy, he's new," she said aloud.

Francine made her way to the side of the building to the staff entrance, where she found the door ajar.

She called out as she entered and closed the door behind her. "Jimmy? It's me, Francine Blake. Where are you? And why'd you leave the door open?"

Francine had expected to see Jimmy waiting and chomping at the bit for her. Most agents were when it came to their dinner relief. Since she didn't know this Jimmy at all, Francine didn't really know what to expect.

"Jimmy. Jimmy!" she called out again.

The cool, well-lit, warehouse-like space with wall-to-wall boxes and crates was massive. Francine knew she would never find Jimmy if he was still out on patrol, so she slowed her pace and headed for the small guards' stand at the front of the museum. Before she could make it to the museum floor entrance, she noticed from the corner of her eye a man sitting slumped over in a chair at a small table. He looked like he was asleep.

"You've got to be kidding me," Francine said out loud, her anger on full display.

Francine made her way over to the table and stood in front of it. "Jimmy! Jimmy, wake up!" she yelled.

When he didn't respond, Francine reached out and tried to shake him. The moment she touched his shoulder, a pain of recognition pierced her heart. Francine quickly checked his pulse…it was weak. She snatched her hand back. Simultaneously, her left hand clutched her cross necklace, and the right hand reached for her gun.

Before Francine could react to what lay before her, a sharp pain pierced her head and darkness suddenly surrounded her.

Meeks walked toward Farrah's office, throwing up his left hand to stop her assistant's protest. While Farrah's office was designed exactly like her sister's, Farrah's furnishings were mostly contemporary. The large oval-shaped curly redwood desk with a turquoise inlay that her sister had made was the focal point of the room. In the area where Francine had chosen to put a sofa, Farrah had placed a six-seat round conference table, made of the same wood, with red leather high-back chairs. Francine's wall of shelves housed mostly books, but Farrah's had a mixture of books, antique art pieces and a small built-in fully stocked bar.

"Farrah, where's Cine?" he demanded. "She's not in her office, and Jeremy said she's out for the rest of the day. I checked upstairs, but she's not there. Is everything okay?" Meeks asked, trying to keep his voice level. "Did she go to the doctor or something?"

"Well, hello to you, too, Meeks…come on in," Farrah said, looking up from the document she'd been reading. "Calm down. Cine's fine. She had some errands to run."

Meeks shifted through a few scenarios in his mind, and

things he could remember that Cine had told him. But if he gauged it correctly, she should have been back in the office by now.

Farrah peered at him a moment, then pushed her long hair that she'd released from its tight bun off her face. Seconds later, she sat back in her chair and intertwined her hands, resting them in her lap.

Robert entered Farrah's office with a determined look on his face. "Morgan's on lockdown. Where's Cine?" he asked.

"Out." Farrah sat up straighter in her chair. "What's going on?"

"Call her…get her back here," Robert said, looking at both Meeks and Farrah.

"I already tried. Her phone's going right to voice mail. What happened?" Meeks asked, fisting his hands at his sides.

"When I went to turn Morgan over to Gary for safekeeping, I heard him murmuring to himself." Robert removed his hat and tossed it in a nearby chair. "He said something to the effect of, *I should never have listened to her. I knew she was crazy.*"

"What's that supposed to mean?" Meeks asked, frowning.

"What the hell's going on?" Farrah demanded as she stood.

Meeks held up his right index finger, and she froze. He needed to concentrate on whatever news Robert was about to deliver.

"I asked that same question, and get this," he said, wiping the sweat from his forehead. "Jasmine brought the Bluebonnet deal to his attention in the first place. She convinced him to *borrow* the money needed for the buy-in from Tiffany. She even helped him set up the dummy accounts so they could keep track of the money they never intended to pay back."

"They?" Meeks asked, frowning.

"Apparently this thing started off as a partnership until Jasmine pulled back," Robert said.

"Yeah, leaving Bill Morgan holding the bag," Meeks said, running his right hand down his face.

"Then she convinced Tiffany to move her security to us…right after the blackmail payments stopped."

"Why?" Meeks asked, a sense of unease settling into his soul.

"Jasmine told him she had unfinished business with someone here. She said that while the bitch in charge—her words, not mine—was useless, the head man over here was brilliant and that this new affiliation could lead to some unique opportunities for both of them…and the greedy bastard fell for it."

Meeks's eyes grew wide with surprise and fear.

Robert's phone beeped. He reached for his cell, which was attached to his belt. Robert slid through a couple of screens and read the message that appeared, and then frowned. "Meeks, our guy at the bank just emailed me Jasmine's financials. You have to see this." He handed the phone over.

Meeks read through the messages. "Shit!"

Farrah had come around her desk and stood between the two men. "Will one of you please tell me what the hell's going on?"

Robert took Farrah's hand and led her over to the conference table across the room, and they both took a seat. He kept their hands intertwined and squeezed hers gently while Meeks walked over to the small bar that was adjacent to the conference table and poured a double shot of the single malt that Farrah stored for stressful occasions like these. He downed his glass, and the smooth taste went to work immediately, filling him with warmth that he hoped would push away the cold feeling that lingered in his fear-ravaged body. He poured glasses for both Robert and Farrah and brought them over to the table.

Meeks took the seat across from Farrah. "Drink," he ordered, handing them each a glass.

Farrah and Robert both downed the brown liquid within seconds. But she slammed her glass to the table. "Now, will one of you please tell me what the hell is going on? I know it's got to be something big if I need a drink *before* you tell me," she said.

Both men took care in bringing Farrah up to speed on everything they had learned and ultimately deduced. Meeks went on to explain to both her and Robert about Jasmine's visit and the things that she'd said.

"So you think Jasmine is behind all of this because she hates my sister and is still all hot and bothered for you?" Farrah said, shaking her head. "Sorry, I just don't think that's a good enough motive. This could be some crazy coincidence."

Meeks sat back in his chair and ran his hands through his hair. "Look, all I know is…Jasmine manipulated her way onto this team, and then she lied to me about her relationship with Tiffany." Meeks dug his right fist into the palm of his left hand. "We have a sophisticated trail leading us to Bill Morgan that she could have easily constructed."

Robert leaned forward and placed his forearms against the table. "My gut tells me she's the one that's been blackmailing Morgan. We just found a bank account in Jasmine's deceased father's name with deposits in the exact amount of the blackmail payments, along with some other rather large deposits that were being made. And since we all know Jergens couldn't have been stalking Tiffany without help, she fits that bill, too."

Farrah started a slow pace around the room as she started French-braiding her hair. "Okay, let's say you're both right about everything. What does she want?"

"Who the hell knows?" Robert said.

Meeks pulled out his phone and tried calling Francine again. "Shit! Why is she still not answering her damn phone?" he said to the room.

"Did you try the apartment?" Robert asked.

"Of course I did!" he snapped. Meeks released a deep sigh. "Track her," he said.

"On it," Robert replied as he pulled out his phone.

"That won't work. She didn't wear her tracking watch," Farrah explained.

"Why the hell not? Where was she going?" Meeks demanded, slamming his fist against the table.

"Roger's kid got sick, and Cine offered to cover his last two stops—the Weinberg School and the Buffalo Soldiers Museum. Since she was only covering breaks and food runs, she didn't think she needed it. After that, she was going to pick up dinner for you two at Jamaica House."

"Did she wear her cross?" Meeks asked, silently praying that she had.

She placed a hand on her hip. "The diamond cross necklace our mom gave us? Of course, she always wears it when she's working. You *know* that."

Meeks looked over at Robert and said, "Call Jeremy for the tracking number and—"

"Wait, you put a tracking device on her necklace...her favorite necklace?" she asked with wide eyes.

Robert nodded his agreement and began dialing on his phone.

"She's going to kill you when she finds out you've been keeping tabs on her. You know that, right?"

"Let's find her first," Meeks answered. "She can kill me later." His forehead creased as he came to a sudden realization. He turned to Farrah. "Wait. Did you say she was going to the Buffalo Soldiers Museum?"

"Yeah, it was one of Roger's last stops," Farrah said with a puzzled look on her face.

"Not possible. We just got a notice that they're moving their business. I haven't had a chance to tell Francine yet. They aren't our clients anymore," he said.

"And the museum is closed for renovations," Robert added. "Did *Roger* tell her to go there?"

"N-no," she stammered.

Everyone moved at once. Both Robert and Meeks followed Farrah, who rushed to the desk and powered up her computer.

"Look," Robert held up his phone. "Roger's last stop was the Weinberg School."

Farrah pulled up the schedule. "Oh, no. The schedule has been altered. The museum had been there until it was removed this morning."

"By who?" Meeks asked as he moved over to the desk and stared down at the screen.

Robert starting dialing Roger.

Farrah tapped several keys, and the screen changed. She looked up at Meeks and said, "You."

"What? I never changed this," Meeks said, fisting his hands at his sides.

"I just confirmed with Roger. His kid wasn't sick and the museum was never on his schedule. He's at the school trying to figure out what happened," Robert said. His phone buzzed and he glanced at the screen. "Found her!"

Meeks snatched the phone from Robert's hand and read the text. He looked at both Farrah and Robert and said, "I'll drive."

Chapter 25

Francine heard someone calling out her name, but she couldn't figure out who it was or where it was coming from. It echoed from a place far away. Her head felt like a marching band had set up residence and was there to stay. The closer the caller got, the louder the band played. No matter how hard she tried, she couldn't make her hands or arms work.

Fighting through the pain, Francine forced her eyes open. She blinked several times in hopes of bringing her sight into focus, but all she could see was a red haze. Her efforts failed, and her eyes closed again. Then a stinging slap registered, causing her eyes to fly open.

"Wakie, wakie, Cine…oh, that's right. It's *Fran*cine," Francine heard the vaguely familiar voice say.

"Who…who are…you?" Francine asked, trying to focus on the voice speaking to her.

"Forgotten me already, have you?" the voice said, laughing.

Francine's blurry vision shifted, but she still couldn't believe what she was seeing—Jasmine, sitting with her legs crossed, casually swinging them back and forth on the same table where Jimmy had been. A handgun, a roll of duct tape and a syringe sat next to her. Francine looked down to find herself seated in a chair. Her hands and feet were bound to the arms and legs of the chair by plastic zip ties. Jimmy was nowhere in sight.

Francine raised her head slowly. While the marching band in her head was still playing, it wasn't as loud, and she was able to think through the pain. She realized that for Jasmine to take things this far, she had to be mentally unstable.

"Jasmine, thank God," Francine said in as frantic of a voice as she could muster. "I don't know what's going on here, but I'm glad you found me. Quick, untie me. Let's get the hell out of here before whoever hit me comes back. Then we can call for backup once we're out of here."

Jasmine's forehead creased before she threw her head back and laughed. "My, my...you are good," she said between laughs. "Or a complete idiot! I'm thinking the latter."

"Jasmine, I don't know what—"

Jasmine jumped off the table and slapped Francine across the face. "Shut the hell up. I'm not stupid and neither are you. You know damn well it was me who knocked you out and tied you to that chair."

Her demeanor had changed into something Francine had never seen before. Her eyes were hard, her nose flared and her jaw clenched; even Jasmine's red hair seemed to have gotten brighter—a shade almost as angry as the woman seemed to be herself. She turned her back to Francine, took a deep breath and released it slowly.

When she turned to face Francine again, the carefree Jasmine had returned.

So much for playing dumb. This chick has lost her mind.

Jasmine hopped back onto the table, crossed her legs again and ran her fingers through her hair. "Now, let's get down to business," she said. "We don't have much time."

"What do you want?" Francine asked, squirming in her chair, trying to break her bindings.

"For you to go away! You're like that annoying sound the smoke detector makes that drives everyone crazy. You damn near have to pull it off the wall to make it stop. " Jasmine said, tilting her head. "Only in this case, it was a bullet."

Francine's breath caught; it was like a shot to the gut, and she shook her head as she realized who was behind the attempt on her life. "No!"

Jasmine laughed. "Yes, Raymond Daniels. Who do you think paid his bail...got him the gun?"

Francine shook her head and said, "You've done all this just to get Meeks back? You can't make a man love you, Jasmine."

Jasmine's smile vanished, and she rolled her eyes. "You really are stupid, aren't you? Yes, Meeks is the reason for this. You're just not good enough for him, but he can't see it. Once you're out of the picture, he and I can get on with the life we were meant to have."

"But he and I weren't even together when you tried to have me killed," Francine explained, trying to buy time. Sooner or later Farrah would figure out that something was wrong, especially since she hadn't returned with her dinner.

"Maybe not officially, but I knew what was happening. I saw the way he looked at you. And then he bought that stupid frame you made. Tried to tell me that it didn't mean anything, that he commissioned a photograph from someone *in Europe* who just happened to have bought it." Jasmine slid off the table with the gun in her hand, walked and stood behind Francine's chair. "If I want a chance at getting Meeks back, I have to get you out of the way."

"You don't have to do this. I'm sure we could come up with another way for you to get what you want," Francine said.

Ignoring Francine's plea, Jasmine bent over and whispered in her ear, "Once you're gone, I'll be on the path to getting what I want…what I deserve. I'll offer my services to help ease things at the office. Then before you know it, I'll be back in Meeks's bed where I belong. Then…and only then, will I have what I want."

Francine knew that her feelings of bewilderment must have shown on her face by the look in Jasmine's eyes and the deep laugh that she released. She continued to ask questions to keep Jasmine's attention on herself and give her time to work on her restraints.

"When I stopped my freelance security work and working the occasional odd job with Meeks, I opened my own firm. However, I started offering more than what the average security agencies offer. I became what you might call a 'problem solver,'" she said as a slow smile spread across her face.

"A problem solver?" Francine asked, but she had already deduced that the woman was no stranger to killing people. She was enjoying this scene a little too much.

"Yes. For example, you're a problem for me that I plan on solving in a few short minutes."

Francine's frown deepened. "You're an assassin?"

Jasmine shivered as though suddenly cold. "Assassin is such a harsh word." Her smile widened, and it caused fear to settle in Francine's gut. She hadn't stalled the woman long enough.

Where the hell is everyone? Francine looked down at her hands and remembered. *Oh, no. I didn't wear the watch… Oh, God! No, stop it…don't panic.*

"You won't get away with this—"

"Shhhh…" Jasmine said, placing her right index finger over her lips. "I already have. I've set everything up. Bill Morgan's going to take the fall for everything. Well… everything except for this, of course."

"You think my sisters, or Meeks for that matter, will just let you walk in and take my place in their lives…just like that?"

"It'll take some time, but I'm sure I'll win them over," she said, giving Francine a little wink. "Besides, I'll only need to deal with your family long enough to get through your funeral. After that, well, let's just say I'll be spending most of my time consoling Meeks. If your family tries to get in my way, they'll just be one more problem for me to solve. And trust me, I'm a very good problem solver."

Keep her talking; you have to save yourself and your baby.

"You know they'll be looking for me," Francine said, fighting the panic building inside her since she knew that they might not be looking for her at all. "They'll never stop trying to find me, to find out what happened to me."

Jasmine dropped her right hand and shifted weight to her right leg. "I'm counting on it. Meeks won't ever move on if you're simply missing. Let me break it down for you, sweetheart." Jasmine leaned forward so she was at eye level with Francine. "This museum is under construction and full of hazardous materials like paint thinner and gasoline. Mix those flammables with some faulty wiring and poof…*problem solved.*"

She straightened and walked back to the table, where she stood and looked over everything that was laid out before her.

"Jasmine, you can't—"

"This place will go up in flames with you inside. You didn't have time to make it out after trying to save poor Jimmy," she said in a sour tone. "Everyone knows how you like to play superhero, so trying to save him on your own won't be a stretch for people to buy."

"Jasmine...please don't...don't do this," Francine said, trying to keep the fear from taking control, or at least keep it out of her voice. Women like Jasmine despised weakness.

Jasmine faced Francine and sighed. "I would say I'm sorry, but...that would be a lie. I want Meeks. As long as you're in the picture, that won't happen."

Francine lowered her tone. "I'll give him up. I'll simply walk away. I won't even try to stop you from...solving your client's problem."

"Stop lying," she yelled. "We both know Meeks is not the type of man a woman can walk away from."

"Jasmine, please—"

"Enough!" Jasmine said as she ripped off a piece of duct tape and placed it over Francine's mouth.

Jasmine stood over Francine and smirked. "This is your own fault, you know," she said, brushing off wood shavings from her clothes. "I tried to make it quick with Daniels. But that didn't work. I'd even planned something very special for you and Tiffany with Lee Jergens, but Meeks stepped in and got you off the case." She grabbed Francine's cheeks with one hand and shook her face. "Now you'll have to die trying to save poor old Jimmy." Then she shrugged. "Oh, well, you saved Tiffany, so that should be some consolation. I really hated the thought of her being collateral damage. At least I was able to finally put that rabid dog Jergens down. He really was one crazy, pathetic piece of a man."

Francine pulled at her bindings, which were too tight for her to slip through. She wanted to scream, but the tape was holding steady. She tried to fight back the tears that began to fill her eyes.

"Time to get this show on the road," Jasmine said as she reached for the syringe. She held it up and flicked it once with her middle finger. "This will help. You'll be out cold, and I'm sure the smoke will take you before the flames get anywhere near you." She smiled, as though she was trying to reassure her. "I've already splattered paint thinner and gasoline all over the place so it shouldn't take long. I moved Jimmy to the storage room where he'll be found. He was a recovering addict and everyone knows how often they slip up, so him having a heroin sandwich at lunch is believable."

Francine's heart sank. She may not have known Jimmy well, but she knew his story. She'd read how he had spent so much time mending his life and his relationship with his family. It pained her that Jasmine was going to take that away from him.

Jasmine stood on the side of Francine. She pushed back Francine's left shoulder with her left hand, holding the syringe in her right hand. "I'd let you have some last words, but I really can't stand the sound of your voice."

Francine's whole body tensed as she lowered her head, closed her eyes and let the tears fall. *I'm sorry, baby. I love you, Meeks. Forgive me, Farrah, Felicia, Mom and Dad.*

"Goodbye, Francine," Jasmine said just before she lowered the needle to Francine's shoulder.

Jasmine suddenly screamed and stumbled backward. The needle crashed to the concrete. "Shit!" she yelled.

Francine flinched at the sound, and her eyes flew open.

She looked up and saw the head of an arrow hanging out of Jasmine's shoulder.

Another arrow whipped through the air. This one landed in Jasmine's upper thigh, and she stumbled again. She released a piercing scream before she dropped to her knees. Jasmine reached for her gun, only to be tackled to the ground by Farrah.

Francine's vision was soon filled with familiar faces. In what felt like seconds, Meeks was kneeling at her right side with his crossbow strapped across his back, slowly removing the duct tape from her mouth.

"Hold on, Cine, we'll get you loose in a second. Just hold on, baby," Meeks said, keeping his focus on her face.

Francine blinked away her tears and nodded.

Seeing Meeks's crossbow, she had assumed he had been the one to shoot Jasmine. That is, until she looked to her left to find her sister kneeling and working to release her hands and feet. Farrah was also wearing her crossbow strapped around her back.

Police, EMS and several of their agents swarmed the room. With both Meeks and her sister by her side and knowing that the baby she carried was safe, Francine could no longer contain her emotions. With her hands and feet finally free, she wrapped her arms around Meeks's neck and cried.

Farrah threw her arms around both Meeks and her sister, kissing her on the cheek as she whispered, "I love you."

"Hey, that's my line," Meeks said.

Francine simply nodded. Meeks tightened his hold on her and said, "I don't know what I would have done if... if we hadn't gotten here in time. I wouldn't have survived losing you."

Chapter 26

After several moments rejoicing in the fact that her sister was safe, Farrah released her hold and walked over to where Robert stood watching over the trio, stopping briefly to check on Jimmy, who was being loaded into a waiting ambulance. Farrah received reassurance that he was going to be fine, then continued toward Robert. Both Robert and Farrah diverted their attention to where the police and their team were working. They watched as EMS treated Jasmine's wounds while she was cuffed to the gurney; she didn't say one word. Because her injuries weren't life threatening and she refused to acknowledge that she understood her rights, the assistant district attorney, a close family friend, had been brought up to speed on all the pending charges and decided not to transport Jasmine until her court-appointed lawyer arrived on the scene and her rights could be reread to her before she was questioned. No one wanted Jasmine to get away with all the things that she'd done.

The police finally removed Jasmine from the warehouse and placed her in another waiting ambulance. The area was marked off and Meeks's team was allowed to videotape and take photos of the warehouse scene as he and Francine watched.

"By the way, nice shot and great call," Robert said, poking Farrah with his elbow.

"Thanks, but it was Meeks. All I could think about was lighting Jasmine's ass up with an arrow straight through that black heart of hers," Farrah said, smiling to herself.

Robert laughed. "I can't believe you actually listened."

"Well, we didn't have much choice," she said, looking around at the cans of paint thinner as well as small puddles of liquid splattered all over the floor. "The moment we opened the door and smelled the paint thinner and gasoline, we knew we couldn't take a chance on firing our guns," she explained.

"Good thing we keep the crossbows in the cars," Robert said.

"Another thing my sister insisted on." Farrah looked over to where Meeks was still holding Francine's hand while EMS was checking her out for any potential injuries. "She could never have known that one day that policy would save her own life."

Farrah and Robert made their way over to where Meeks and Francine were standing. Meeks was conferring with the EMS attendant who had just cleared Francine to leave, who recommended that she follow up with her own doctor in a day or two.

Robert pulled Francine into a brief hug. "You okay?"

Francine kept her hold on Meeks's hand. "I am now," she said, smiling up at Meeks and then at her sister.

"I spoke to Sergeant Jefferson, and he's willing to come to your place in the morning to take your statements. He has enough here to keep himself busy, so you can take her home," Robert explained to both Meeks and Francine.

"Thanks," Francine replied.

"We'll handle everything on this end," Robert said, turning his gaze toward Farrah.

Farrah nodded and gifted Robert with a slow, sexy smile.

"Sergeant Jefferson is going to question Bill Morgan about his role in this mess and we'll bring Tiffany up to speed on everything, too. At least she doesn't have anything else to worry about now," Farrah said.

"I think we should keep a team on her for a little while longer anyway, just to be sure," Francine declared.

"Will do," Robert said.

"Thanks, man…for everything." Meeks and Robert shook hands while the sisters shared an embrace.

Meeks circled his arm around Francine's waist. "You ready to go?" Meeks asked.

"Yes," she said, leaning into Meeks's chest. "I'm ready to go home."

"Please, baby, I know what the EMS said, but let me have Dr. Perry meet us at home to check you out…for me," he said, his eyes begging for her compliance.

"Home…okay," she whispered.

Meeks scooped Francine up into his arms. "Hey!" she protested. "I can walk. Besides, I want to go thank the guys again."

"Woman, I'm not letting you out of my sight, and you've already thanked them. Anything else can wait."

Carrying Francine in his arms, Meeks walked outside and headed toward his truck.

From her gurney in the ambulance, Jasmine screamed Meeks's name over and over. Francine's whole body tensed.

Meeks pulled her closer to his chest and smiled down at her as if he hadn't heard Jasmine's call.

He kissed Francine lightly on the lips and whispered, "I love you."

She buried her face in Meeks's neck and said, "I love you, too."

Chapter 27

Francine sat on her sofa wrapped in an oversize white robe, trying to comprehend all she'd learned and shared over the past twenty-four hours. Between what Meeks, Robert and her sister had told her about Jasmine and everything she'd learned on her own about the woman, Francine was feeling tired and overwhelmed. However, through it all, she'd made a couple of decisions that she needed to share with Meeks. Well, almost everything. Francine decided to keep her position of power within the company—thanks to the proxies she now controlled—to herself.

Meeks walked over to Francine, wearing his matching white robe, and handed her a coffee mug. "Here you go. Tea with lemon and honey," Meeks said, sitting down next to her on the sofa.

"Thanks," she said, taking a sip and sighing as the warmth spread within her. "That's good."

Meeks pushed Francine's hair off her shoulders, leaned over and kissed her on the corner of her mouth. She closed her eyes and smiled. A flash of the two of them making love the night before and just now in the shower flashed through her mind. Her body responded to his touch like always, but Francine knew she had to refrain—just for a little while longer.

"Meeks, we have to talk," Francine said, placing her cup on the table.

"What's up?" Meeks asked, rubbing her back with his right hand.

"About the board meeting."

Meeks sighed and dropped his hand. "Sweetheart, I understand how you feel, but I can't back down from this. Personal security for celebrities, it's just not—"

"I know," she said, smiling.

Meeks's expression froze, and Francine's smile widened.

"You *know*? What do you know?"

"I know about that bug you had placed on my necklace," she said, crossing her legs and folding her arms.

Meeks gave her a guilty smile.

"Farrah told me about it when she called to check on me this morning."

"I can explain that—"

"And I can't wait to hear it," she cut in. "Later. Right now, I want to tell you about a couple of decisions I've made. First, I can't say I agree with you one hundred percent, but I can see everyone's point about the celebrity aspect of our business, so I propose a compromise." Francine lowered her arms.

"Compromise…like what?" Meeks asked with a raised eyebrow.

"We limit our celebrity personal protection offerings to products and monitoring services only. There are plenty of agencies and freelancers out there that can handle the bodyguard aspect of things. We can even provide them with a few quality references."

Meeks took her hands in his and smiled. "I think that's a brilliant idea. And your second decision?"

Francine could see the hope in Meeks's eyes. She'd weighed out her idea of having it all and what that meant for her versus her mother. "I think it's time I stepped back from fieldwork and embrace the CEO role as my father intended—unless I'm needed, of course."

Meeks's relief was almost tangible.

"Not to mention focusing a little more time and attention on a very pushy man who thinks he's going to marry me," Francine said, picking up her tea and taking a sip as she looked at him over the rim of her cup.

Meeks laughed, and his eyes sparked with excitement. "Oh, I can think of several things you're needed for other than fieldwork," he said, grabbing at her and trying to untie her robe. "And I already told you, marrying me is a done deal."

Francine laughed as she melted into him, loosening his robe. "You really suck at the whole proposal thing, you know."

"Just wait, but in the meantime..." he said, stopping her hands. Meeks stood and tightened the belt on his robe. "How about I get us something stronger than tea to drink to celebrate our *compromise*?"

Francine stood and stopped his progress. She intertwined their hands and held his gaze. "Nothing for me. Well, at least not for another seven and a half months..."

Meeks's jaw dropped as he just stared at her.

"With everything that's happened, I hadn't had a chance to tell you," she said, breaking eye contact and looking down at their joined hands.

Meeks withdrew his right hand, used his index finger

to raise her head and stared into her eyes. "Tell me now. I want to hear you say the words."

Francine smiled as she watched his eyes glaze over with unshed tears. "We're having a baby."

Meeks pulled Francine into his arms and kissed her breathless. "I love you," he said after letting her up for air.

Francine laughed. "I love you, too."

Meeks dropped down on one knee, stared up into Francine's eyes and held their interwoven hands at his heart. "I don't have a ring to offer right now, but I do have my life, my heart…my soul, and they're yours. Would you be willing to share them with me?"

The overwhelming feelings of love and passion Francine felt for Meeks in that moment were nearly too much to handle. She had to flex all her muscles just to stay upright. "Now *that's* a proposal," she said, smiling down at him as the tears began to flow.

He stood and leaned in to kiss her tears away as he said, "Finally, I get something right."

* * * * *

This summer is going to be hot, hot, hot
with a new miniseries
from fan-favorite authors!

YAHRAH ST. JOHN
LISA MARIE PERRY
PAMELA YAYE

HEAT WAVE OF DESIRE	HOT SUMMER NIGHTS	HEAT OF PASSION
Available June 2015	*Available July 2015*	*Available August 2015*

California Desert Dreams

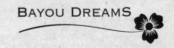

REQUEST YOUR FREE BOOKS!

2 FREE NOVELS
PLUS 2 FREE GIFTS!

KIMANI™
ROMANCE

Love's ultimate destination!

YES! Please send me 2 FREE Harlequin® Kimani™ Romance novels and my 2 FREE gifts (gifts are worth about $10). After receiving them, if I don't wish to receive any more books, I can return the shipping statement marked "cancel." If I don't cancel, I will receive 4 brand-new novels every month and be billed just $5.44 per book in the U.S. or $5.99 per book in Canada. That's a savings of at least 16% off the cover price. It's quite a bargain! Shipping and handling is just 50¢ per book in the U.S. and 75¢ per book in Canada.* I understand that accepting the 2 free books and gifts places me under no obligation to buy anything. I can always return a shipment and cancel at any time. Even if I never buy another book, the two free books and gifts are mine to keep forever.

168/368 XDN GH4P

Name	(PLEASE PRINT)
Address	Apt. #
City	State/Prov.	Zip/Postal Code

Signature (if under 18, a parent or guardian must sign)

Mail to the **Reader Service:**
IN U.S.A.: P.O. Box 1867, Buffalo, NY 14240-1867
IN CANADA: P.O. Box 609, Fort Erie, Ontario L2A 5X3

Want to try two free books from another line?
Call 1-800-873-8635 or visit www.ReaderService.com.

* Terms and prices subject to change without notice. Prices do not include applicable taxes. Sales tax applicable in N.Y. Canadian residents will be charged applicable taxes. Offer not valid in Quebec. This offer is limited to one order per household. Not valid for current subscribers to Harlequin® Kimani™ Romance books. All orders subject to credit approval. Credit or debit balances in a customer's account(s) may be offset by any other outstanding balance owed by or to the customer. Please allow 4 to 6 weeks for delivery. Offer available while quantities last.

Your Privacy—The Reader Service is committed to protecting your privacy. Our Privacy Policy is available online at www.ReaderService.com or upon request from the Reader Service.

We make a portion of our mailing list available to reputable third parties that offer products we believe may interest you. If you prefer that we not exchange your name with third parties, or if you wish to clarify or modify your communication preferences, please visit us at www.ReaderService.com/consumerchoice or write to us at Reader Service Preference Service, P.O. Box 9062, Buffalo, NY 14240-9062. Include your complete name and address.

KROM15

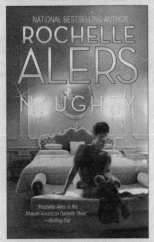

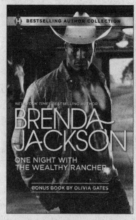